Investigations of a Dog
and other creatures

OTHER BOOKS BY AND ABOUT KAFKA

from New Directions

Franz Kafka, *Amerika*

Gustav Janouch, *Conversations with Kafka*

Reiner Stach, *Is That Kafka?*

INVESTIGATIONS OF A DOG

and other creatures

Franz Kafka

in a new translation by Michael Hofmann

A NEW DIRECTIONS PAPERBOOK ORIGINAL

Published by arrangement with Penguin Books Ltd., London.

First published as a New Directions Paperbook (NDP1377) in 2017
Manufactured in the United States of America
New Directions Books are printed on acid-free paper
Design by Erik Rieselbach

Library of Congress Cataloging-in-Publication Data
Names: Kafka, Franz, 1883–1924, author. | Hofmann, Michael, 1957 August 25– translator.
Title: Investigations of a dog, and other creatures / Franz Kafka ; translated and with an introduction by Michael Hofmann.
Description: New York : New Directions Publishing Corporation, 2017.
Identifiers: LCCN 2017008606 | ISBN 9780811226899 (alk. paper)
Subjects: LCSH: Kafka, Franz, 1883–1924—Translations into English. | Short stories, German—Translations into English.
Classification: LCC PT2621.A26 A2 2017 | DDC 833/.912—dc23
LC record available at https://lccn.loc.gov/2017008606

10 9 8 7 6 5 4 3 2 1

New Directions Books are published for James Laughlin
by New Directions Publishing Corporation
80 Eighth Avenue, New York 10011

Contents

A note on the text

The present translations were made from the volume *Die Erzählungen und andere ausgewählte Prosa* (S. Fischer, 1996), edited by Roger Hermes; the texts are from the 1982 manuscript edition, prepared by Jürgen Born, Gerhard Neumann, Malcolm Pasley, and Jost Schillemeit.

Because the emphasis is on stories, some early work ("Wedding Preparations in the Country," "Description of a Struggle," "The First Long Train Journey" (toward "Richard and Samuel," cowritten with Max Brod)), playlets ("The Warden of the Tomb"), and aphorisms (the "Collected" or "Zürau" aphorisms from 1917 and the 1920 sequence known as "He") are not included. The order attempts the chronological.

Only a few of the pieces were given titles by Kafka; the rest of the titles, mostly Brod's, are those in square brackets on the contents page. A number of the pieces end rather abruptly, in mid-sentence or mid-punctuation. Again, Brod sought to smooth these out; in the present edition, they are left as they were, rough.

M.H.

Foreword

With few, brief, circumstantial exceptions (illness, Christmas, visits to rustic spas and sanatoria), Kafka worked in the daytime and wrote at night (see the little piece bearing that name: "Night"). He devised for himself a life that was largely disagreeable, inflexible, and inescapable, and tried to make it productive. Never remotely trusting himself to write for a living, he held down a demanding and increasingly responsible job for the Workers' Accident Insurance Institute for the Kingdom of Bohemia, from 1908 to 1922, almost his entire adult life. Unable to commit himself to a wife in spite of three engagements—to Felice Bauer in June 1914 and again in July 1917, and to Julie Wohryzek in summer 1919—and a few not-so-near Misses, he lived, for the most part, with his unsympathetic parents, in the difficult city of Prague, an aging bachelor of habits both confirmed and challenging (see the stories "Blumfeld, an Elderly Bachelor" and "The Married Couple," but also those like "Hunter Gracchus" and "Visiting the Dead" about an indeterminate condition half-alive, half-dead, that may well be a version of bachelordom). There was never anything in Kafka's life that approached the categorical importance of writing (it would, in his word, *capsize* anything else he did), but just for that it had to wait its turn:

> from 8 to 2 or 2:30 in the office, then lunch till 3 or 3:30, after that sleep in bed (usually only attempts ...) till 7:30, then ten minutes of exercises, naked at the open window, then an hour's walk—alone, with Max, or with another friend, then dinner with my family (I have three sisters, one married, one engaged; the single one, without prejudicing my affection for the others, is easily my favorite); then at 10:30 (but often not till 11:30) I sit down to write, and I go on, depending on my strength, inclination, and luck, until 1, 2, or 3 o'clock, once even until 6 in the morning. Then again exercises, as above, but of course avoiding all exertions, a wash, and then, usually with a slight pain in my heart and twitching stomach muscles, to bed. (*Letters to Felice*, Schocken Books, 1988, p. 22, letter of November 1, 1912).

he wrote, wooingly, or perhaps in lieu of wooing, to Felice. The complacencies of Pepys it isn't. At the same time, though, it is clear that Kafka understands that anything (independence, moving house, marriage) undertaken, in thought or deed, in opposition to such a routine will be seen primarily as an attack on—of all things—his writing (which is the thing that is under attack from everything else). The upstream dam threatens not just the river, but the boulder under the river. You can feel the defensive bristle of the arrangement—not least as the writing is so intricately, almost magically circumstantial, profoundly depending on such scanty outward events in Kafka's uneventful life as correspondence, engagements, and house moves (the always representative story "The Judgment" was written two nights after Felice replied to his first letter; Elias Canetti's book *Kafka's Other Trial: The Letters to Felice* maps in fascinating detail the way the vicissitudes of the novel follow the vicissitudes of their first engagement). Writing hid, trembling, and awaited the pleasure of *force majeure*, which came, ultimately, in the form of Kafka's fatal (though also, he wrote, "beckoned to") illness, which announced itself in 1917, when he suffered the pulmonary hemorrhage that was the first sure indication of his tuberculosis.

Kafka's writing dramatizes a continual dialectic of strength and weakness, usually in unexpected forms and with unexpected outcomes. Instability is all. The helmsman is straightforwardly overwhelmed by a rival; the crew lets it happen. The messenger in "A Message from the Emperor" is described as "a strong man, tireless, a champion swimmer" but he has no chance of even making it out of the imperial palace. The whole of China is ruled by one man, though he may have been dead for hundreds of years. The god Poseidon hates his public image—salt spray, chest hair, and trident—and dreams of a break and a cruise. Out of fear, anxiety, and calamity, writing is spun that is as supple and cogent and unbroken as one would imagine only an expression of radiant triumphalism and certitude could be. Throughout his life, Kafka thought of himself as weak. "The world [...] and I in insoluble conflict have torn apart my body." His body—His Majesty, the Body, he ironically stylized it—would not do the things he asked of it, principally write, in spite of the daily open-air exercises and such things as rowing, swimming, carpentering, and gardening. "Nothing can be accomplished with such a body," he wrote in his habitual categorical way; though a fairer observer, his biographer Klaus Wagenbach, describes him justly and every bit as categorically, as "a strikingly beautiful, slender, tall man, with nothing of the hermit about him." An unusually physical approach to writing (and to life) left him ridiculously vulnerable. Everything is in his writing; nothing is anywhere else:

> It is easy to recognize a concentration in me of all my forces on writing. When it became clear in my organism that writing was the most productive direction for my being to take, everything rushed in that direction and left empty all those abilities that were directed toward the joys of sex, eating, drinking, philosophical reflection, and above all music. This was necessary because the totality of my strengths was so light that only collectively could they even halfway serve the purpose of writing. (*The Diaries of Franz Kafka, 1910–1913*, Schocken Books, 1988, p. 163.)

It was at night that his weaknesses were at their strongest and his strength at its weakest. Often in his diaries he talks of writing in, or writing himself into, a state of unconsciousness. This could be miraculous, as it was on September 22, 1912, the night he wrote the story, "*Das Urteil*" ("The Judgment"), which, to the end of his life, stood for the way these things should be done; but it could also be unpredictable, subject to revision, to disappointment, or to shame. "Even night is not night enough," wrote Kafka. Night is a pocketful of change in front of a fruit machine; it has no optics, no prudence, and no settled opinion. Things done at night are regularly menaced by incompleteness or immoderateness, and by a change of heart or change of mind. The great Swedish poet Tomas Tranströmer writes about his own experience, but it's the same thing (in the poem "Baltics," the translator is Patty Crane):

You might wake up during the night
and quickly throw some words down
on the nearest paper, in the margins of the news
(the words radiant with meaning!)
but in the morning: the same words don't say anything,
   scribbles, slips of the tongue.
Or fragments of the great nightly writing that drew past?

Tranströmer has a vastly different tone from Kafka, an easy irony, an easy wisdom, an easy relativism; he knows, as Kafka endearingly seems not to, that things look different in the morning. (Inexplicably and wonderfully, just below the lines quoted, he has "They set up his student K as the head prosecutor.") Still, Kafka or not, these "fragments of the great nightly writing that drew past" (since I read it, the phrase wouldn't let me go) is precisely what we have in *Investigations of a Dog.*

Kafka always wrote in jags or streaks, and then for months or years little or nothing that survived. His last companion, Dora Diamant, with whom he lived, dying, in Berlin, thinks he wrote "The Burrow" in one night, or at least the greater part of it. All the stories collected here are the product of three or four "hot" phases—mostly clustered around its longer pieces—in 1917, in 1922, and in the winter of 1923-4. But it was ever thus. He wrote two drafts of *Amerika/The Man Who Disappeared* in a matter of weeks each; he wrote *The Trial* in the space of a few months in 1914; similarly *The Castle* in 1922; and abandoned each of them. His production was hectic, excessive, fiercely doubted, or it was nothing. It also had a tendency to double up against itself. Kafka interrupted *Amerika* for three weeks in November 1912 to deliver himself of *Metamorphosis*; he similarly suspended work on *The Trial* for eleven days—nights—and wrote "In the Penal Colony" and the final "Oklahoma" chapter of *Amerika*. He is like a painter—he is like Max Beckmann, who worked at night, by artificial light, and from what you might call a real imagination—who either paints nothing, or works on several canvases at once.

Night offers a seeming monopoly of consciousness; a certain self-aware solipsism; strange auditory conditions; sensitivity to light; Bengal noon for the nerves. A mixture of heightening and deadening, of privacy and vulnerability. Spatial relations are unclear, sensory prompts unpredictable, immediate, oddly, even frighteningly effective (perhaps "The Silence of the Sirens," certainly "The Burrow"). Oscar's friend Franz in the first story here, "In the City," rubs his eyes with his two little fingers, and later scratches at his throat behind the goatee beard, "in that closer intimacy one has with one's body after sleep," as Kafka sumptuously puts it. Night is organic, is appetite and fear, is the day of (a phrase I love) the "regulation dog." It is creatureliness and mystery: "tears of joy and relief still glitter in the hairs of my beard when I awake." Fighting and eating—the simple creature dreamily asserting itself—are never so much desired as they are here in Kafka—not even by Hemingway. It is when the unnamed, unspecified denizen of the burrow (come in, Vladimir Nabokov) on the one hand has a thrilling, visceral fear of "the pursuer's teeth clamped on my thighs," and on the other yearns for free passage, "then at last I could run at him"—a different him—"free of all concerns I could leap at him, bite him, tear his flesh, chew it and drain his blood and cram his carcass down there with the rest of the quarry."

Kafka's subjects here are largely businessmen and beasts, either paired ("The Village Schoolmaster," "Blumfeld, an Elderly Bachelor") or separately (on the one hand "My Business" or "The Married Couple"; on the other, "A Cross-Breed" or "Investigations of a Dog"). (Agreeably, in "Advocates," the two tropes are momentarily run together: "the prosecutors, those wily foxes, those nippy weasels, those invisible voles slip through the smallest crannies and whisk through between the feet of the advocates.") In either case, it is a markedly depleted, technical sort of life, beset with imperatives and hierarchies and limitations ("The Married Couple," "Investigations of a Dog," "The Burrow").

Family stories—"The Judgment," *Metamorphosis*, "The Stoker: A Fragment"—tended to be the ones that were drawn out for publication, in the seven short books that Kafka agreed to have published in his lifetime, collected in English as *Metamorphosis and Other Stories*. The pieces here are outlying, perhaps the outer, wilder ripples ("Little Fable") of Kafka's disturbance. Thus "In the City" is like an earlier version of "The Judgment"; "It Was One Summer" stands in some relation both to "A Country Doctor" and "In the Penal Colony." Such pieces as "Building the Great Wall of China" or "Our Little Town" or "Our City Coat of Arms" comment on a kind of empire-feeling (after all, Kafka was named Franz by his parents after the Emperor Franz Joseph), a strange apathy, often ignorance or disengagement: "like strangers in a city, like latecomers, they stand at the back of densely crowded side streets, calmly eating their packed lunches, while a long way in front of them on the market square the execution of their overlord is in progress." Piranesian structures, great and small walls, corridors, courtyards, staircases, Towers of Babel await occupation. "I require silence in my passageways," says the animal in "The Burrow," sounding strangely introspective, as if for an ECG or a sonogram. Chaos, starvation—

lightheadedness, lightbodiedness—and plain dread menace these structures, or hauntingly—think of Kafka's TB—all their intricacies are leveled, swept aside by a tide of blood, as in the terrifyingly equivocal ending of "The Vulture": "Now I saw that he had understood everything, he flew up, leaning right back to get plenty of momentum, and then, like a javelin thrower, he thrust his beak through my mouth deep into me. As I fell back, I could feel a sense of deliverance as he wallowed and drowned in the blood that now filled all my vessels and burst its banks." They break off in brittleness and suggestion, like "Night"; they exhaust their idea like "Little Fable" or "Poseidon"; or they weirdly and tenaciously adhere, like the "Investigations of a Dog" or "The Burrow."

Camus, in one of the places where he sounds most like Kafka—endlessly surprising, endlessly provocative, endlessly serene, the unmoved Mover—says: "One should think of Sisyphus as happy." Something about the making of these tumultuous stones—or stories—strikes me nonetheless as exquisitely happy.

MICHAEL HOFMANN
HAMBURG, JUNE 2016

Investigations of a Dog
and other creatures

In the City

One winter's afternoon, during a blizzard, Oscar M., an aging student—if you looked at him from close up, you saw that he had terrifying eyes—Oscar M., in winter clothes and winter coat, scarf around his neck and a fur hat on his head, came to a sudden stop on the empty square. Whatever he was thinking was causing his eyes to blink rapidly. He was sunk so deep in thought that at one point he took off his hat and rubbed its coarse fur against his face. Finally he seemed to come to a conclusion, spun on his heel like a dancer, and headed home. When he opened the door of his parents' apartment, he saw his father, a fleshy-faced, clean-shaven man, sitting at an empty table facing the door. "Not before time," he said, no sooner had Oscar set foot in the room, "and not a step closer, please, I am so furious with you that I can't answer for the consequences." "But Father," said Oscar, and only then did he notice that he was all out of breath. "Quiet!" yelled his father, and stood up, obscuring a window. "Quiet, I say. And but me no buts, all right?" So saying, he picked up the table in his two hands and carried it one pace nearer to Oscar. "I can't put up with your dissolute life a moment longer. I am an old man. I thought to have in

3

you a support for my later years, but you've turned out to be worse than my illnesses. I'm disgusted by such a son, who by sheer laziness, prodigality, wickedness, and stupidity is driving his old father to an early grave."

At this point the old man fell silent, though his face continued to work as though he was still speaking. "Dear Papa," said Oscar, and cautiously approached the table, "calm yourself, everything will be all right. I have just had an idea that will make me the productive human being of your dreams." "What's that, then?" asked his father, staring fixedly into a corner. "Trust me, I'll explain it to you over supper. Really, I was always a good son, only the fact that I wasn't able to prove it to you so embittered me that, seeing that I was unable to delight you, I chose to annoy you instead. But now just let me take a turn in the fresh air to help me develop my thoughts." His father, who had initially been leaning against the table in growing attentiveness, stood up: "I don't believe what you've just said is worth much. It's just talk. But in the end you are my son. Come back soon, we'll eat together, and you can tell me what's on your mind." "That small indication of your confidence is enough for me. I thank you for it sincerely. But isn't it apparent from my expression that I'm completely taken up with this serious plan?" "I don't know about that," said his father. "Perhaps it's my fault, I've rather got out of the habit of looking at you at all." And so saying, it was a habit of his, he tapped on the table to indicate the passing of time. "The principal thing is that I have no confidence left in you, Oscar. If I yelled at you—I yelled at you when you came in, didn't I?—then it wasn't in any hope that it might improve you, I only did it thinking of your poor Mama, who, while she may not yet feel any pain over you, is already being weakened by her efforts to ward off such a pain (she thinks this is somehow in your interests). But in the end these are all things that you know very well, and I would have saved myself the trouble of mentioning them to you again, had you not provoked me with your promises."

In the midst of these latest words the maid entered the room to see to the stove. No sooner had she left again than Oscar exclaimed: "But Papa! I would never have looked to you for such forbearance. If I'd had just a small idea, let's say something toward my dissertation, which has been languishing in my bookcase these past ten years and is desperately in need of fresh ideas, then it's just about possible, if hardly likely, that I would have come running home from my walk as happened today, and said, Father, I've had an idea. And if you had thereupon, with your respected voice, repeated your reproaches of a moment ago, then my idea would have been simply blown away and I should have had no option but to march off with or without a word of apology. Whereas now! Everything you say in objection to me helps my ideas—they don't stop coming, they multiply and grow in my head. I will go now, because I need to be alone to put them in some order." He gulped for breath in the warm room. "Of course it could be some villainy you've got in your head," said his father with big, round eyes, "then I believe it would indeed get you in its grip. If it's any kind of decent thought, though, it'll disappear overnight. I know you." Oscar twisted his head, as though someone had him by the throat. "That's enough. You're picking away at me for no reason. The mere possibility that you might be able to predict the outcome accurately shouldn't tempt you to disturb me in my good thoughts. Perhaps my past record gives you the right to do something like that, but it's still wrong of you to make use of it."

"That only goes to show how great your uncertainty must be, if you are compelled to talk to me like that." "Nothing compels me," said Oscar, and his head gave a twitch. He went right up to the table, so that it was no longer possible to tell whose it was. "What I said, I said with respect and even with love for you, as you will see in due course, because my regard for you and Mama plays a leading role in my idea." "In that case I'd probably better thank you now," said his father, "seeing that it's most unlikely that your mother and I will still be among the living when the proper time for thanks comes round." "Please, Father, let the future rest, as it deserves. If you wake it ahead of time, the only result is a sleepy-headed present. You shouldn't need your son to remind you of that. Also, I wasn't about to try and persuade you of anything, I was just announcing my idea. And that at least, as even you will have to admit, I've succeeded in doing."

"Now, Oscar, one thing still perplexes me: how is it that you've not come to me more often with such things? It accords so much with your nature. No, no, I'm serious."

"Well, if only you'd given me a good beating instead of listening to me. I came running here, God knows, to give you a pleasant surprise. But as long as my plan isn't wholly thought through, I can't tell you what it is. So why punish me for my good intentions and demand explanations of me that will only impede the execution of my plan?"

"That's enough now. I'm not interested anyway. But I had better tell you, because I can see you retreating to the door, obviously in some tearing rush to get somewhere: by your little device you have managed to allay the worst of my rage, with the result that I merely feel sadder than I did before, so I would like to beg you—if you like, I'll even fold my hands like this—at least not to breathe a word about your ideas to your mother. Be satisfied with me."

"This is not my father who's speaking to me in this way," cried Oscar, his hand already on the doorknob. "Either something's happened to you since midday or you're a stranger, someone I've never met before, in my father's stead. My true father"—for an instant Oscar stopped openmouthed—"would have thrown his arms around me, he would have summoned my mother to come. What's the matter with you, Father?"

"I suggest you go and eat with your true father then. It promises to be much more agreeable."

"He will come, give him time. He can't fail. And Mother will be there too. And Franz, whom I'm going to fetch now. Everyone!" And with that Oscar barged into the door, as though to force it open, though it swung effortlessly.

Once he'd arrived at Franz's lodgings, he bent down to the little landlady with the words, "It's all right, the engineer is asleep, I know," and without paying any attention to the woman who, unhappy in view of the late visit, continued to pace uselessly back and forth in the corridor, he opened the glass door which shuddered as though he had touched it at some sensitive spot and called out boldly into the middle of the room which was almost completely dark: "Franz, get up! I need your advice. But I don't want to stay here, I want to take a walk. Also I want you to come and eat with us. So hurry up." "At your service," came the reply from the engineer on his leather sofa, "but what are we doing first—getting up, eating, walking or advising? I expect there are some other things I'm overlooking as well." "Above all, Franz, no jokes. That's the most important thing of all, I forgot to say." "Well, I can oblige. But as for getting up—I'd rather eat twice on your behalf than get up once." "Now, up you get! No resistance." Oscar grabbed his friend by the lapels and pulled him into a sitting position.

"I say, you do mean it, don't you. Respect." He rubbed his eyes with both little fingers. "Tell me, has anyone ever bodily lifted you off a sofa like that?" "Go on, Franz," said Oscar with a grimace, "go on and get dressed. I'm not an idiot to go waking you for no reason." "Nor am I an idiot for sleeping with no reason either. I was on night shift yesterday, and I missed out on my afternoon nap today as well, on account of you." "What?" "Oh, I'm just annoyed by how little attention you pay me. Not for the first time either. Of course, you're a student with no commitments, free to do as you please. Not everyone's so lucky. Then surely to goodness you have to pay a bit of respect to others. I am your friend, but that's not what keeps me in my job." He demonstrated by waving the palms of his hands about in the air. "Doesn't the eloquence rather suggest that you've had more than enough sleep," said Oscar, who was braced against a bedpost, from where he eyed the engineer as though he had more time than before.

"What do you want me to do? Or, if you like, why did you wake me up?" asked the engineer, scratching at his throat behind the goatee beard, in that closer intimacy one has with one's body after sleep. "What I want you to do," said Oscar, tapping the bed frame with his heel. "Very little. I told you what it was from the corridor: to get dressed." "If you mean to suggest by that, Oscar, that your news is of very little interest to me, then I'm bound to say you're right."

"So much the better, because in that case the fire it will

light in you will be lit all by itself, and won't rely on our friendship at all. Your advice will be clearer too. I need clear advice, please bear that in mind. And now if you happen to be looking for your collar and tie, they're on the chair." "Why, thank you," said the engineer, beginning to put them on. "Perhaps you are a reliable person after all."

The Village Schoolmaster

Those, and I count myself among them, who find an ordinary mole disgusting, would probably have died of disgust if they had seen the giant mole that was spotted a few years ago in the vicinity of a small village which thereby gained a measure of fleeting fame. Now, admittedly, it's long since sunk back into obscurity, like the whole episode, which has remained a riddle, not that any very great efforts have been undertaken to explain it, and which—as a consequence of the baffling neglect of precisely those minds that should have devoted themselves to it, but instead devoted their energy to the explanation of things of much less consequence—has been forgotten for want of a detailed investigation. The fact that the village is a long way from any train line can hardly serve as an excuse. Many people came there out of curiosity from far away, some even from abroad; yet those who should have showed a little more than curiosity failed to come. Yes, if it hadn't been for ordinary people, people whose daily lives barely gave them a moment to catch their breath, if it hadn't been for the selfless efforts of such people, then the rumor of the phenomenon would probably have scarcely left the confines of the parish. It should be admitted that even rumor, something ordinarily so hard to brake, in this particular instance was positively sluggish, and if it hadn't been given a nudge or two, it might never have got going at all. But not even that was any reason not to take time with this phenomenon; the thing simply deserved to have been investigated.

Instead of which, the only written account was left to an old village schoolmaster, an excellent man in his profession, no question, but whose gifts, like his training, were hardly such as to permit him to offer so much as a basic description, much less any explanation. His treatise was printed and sold in many copies to the then inhabitants of the village, where it met with a measure of praise, but the teacher was sensible enough to see that his isolated and unsupported efforts were basically valueless. If he nevertheless chose to persist in them and made of the affair, in spite of its annually increasing obscurity, his life's work, then that goes to prove, on the one hand, the importance the phenomenon might have had, and on the other, the degree of stamina and unwavering conviction that can be found in an old unregarded schoolmaster.

The fact that he suffered badly from his rejection by influential parties is demonstrated by a short postscript he appended to his monograph, admittedly after an interval of some years, at a time, therefore, when hardly anyone could remember the original matter. In this postscript he attacks—his accusation hardly persuasive by its deftness, but by its honesty—the incomprehension he met with in people where it should have least been expected. Of these people he remarks aptly: "It is they, not I, who talk like an old village schoolmaster." And he cites, among other things, the reaction of an expert whom he sought out in the matter.

The expert is not named, but it is not difficult to guess his identity. After the schoolmaster had overcome great difficulties to gain admission from the expert, to whom he had announced his visit several weeks previously, he noticed from the moment of their meeting that the expert harbored invincible prejudices regarding the affair. The degree of inattention with which he heard the lengthy report the schoolmaster made on the basis of his monograph may be judged by a remark he passed after some apparent pause for reflection.

"Yes, moles come in all types and sizes. There where you live, the earth is especially rich and black. Well, it stands to reason that the nutrition it gives to moles will be especially abundant, and it's only to be expected that they will grow to an unusual size." "But not as big as that!" exclaimed the schoolmaster, and exaggerating a little in his rage, he paced off some seven feet along the wall. "Oh, yes," said the expert, to whom the whole business obviously felt a little ridiculous, "why ever not?" Thus snubbed, the schoolmaster went home. He tells how, that evening in the falling snow, his wife and six children came to meet him on the road, and he was compelled to acknowledge the final failure of all his hopes.

At the time I read about this treatment afforded to the schoolmaster, I was not yet acquainted with his opus. But I decided straightaway to collect and assemble all the materials I could in the case. Since I could hardly shake my fist in the expert's face, I wanted my writing at the very least to speak up for the schoolmaster, or, better, not the schoolmaster per se so much as the good intentions of an honest man with little influence. I will admit I later regretted this decision, because I soon came to feel that putting it into effect could not but put me in a false position. On the one hand, my own influence was hardly such as to be able to bring the expert, much less public opinion on the whole, round to the teacher's views; on the other, the teacher was bound to notice that I was less concerned with his principal goal, the proof of the appearance of the giant mole, than with the unasked-for defense of his good name, which would seem to him to stand in no need of my defense.

So, as was bound to happen, in seeking to associate myself with the teacher, I met with his incomprehension, and probably instead of helping, soon stood in need of a new helper myself, whose appearance on the scene was highly unlikely. Moreover, my engagement on his behalf involved me in a great deal of work. If I wanted to convince people, I couldn't rely on the teacher who, it seemed, had little power to convince. Knowledge of his monograph would only have muddied the water, and I therefore avoided reading it until my own work was completed. I didn't even get in touch with him. Of course, through intermediaries, he got to hear of my inquiries, but he had no idea whether I was with him or against him. He perhaps thought the latter, though he was to deny this later on, because I have proof that he tried to put obstacles in my path. This was not at all difficult for him, seeing as I was obliged to carry out all the investigations he had already conducted, and he was able to anticipate me at every turn. But this was the only objection that could reasonably be made to my approach; an unavoidable objection, and limited as much as possible by the self-denying scrupulousness of my conclusions. Other than that, my paper was free of any influence on the part of the teacher; it is possible I was even overscrupulous in this regard. It really was as though no one had yet investigated the case at all, as though I were the first to interview the witnesses, the first to collate the accounts, the first to draw conclusions.

When I subsequently read the teacher's treatise—it had the terribly cumbersome title: A Mole Larger Than Any Yet Seen—I found a number of differences, even though we both thought we had proved our main thesis, which is to say the mole's existence. Still, odd points of difference between us got in the way of the friendly relationship with the teacher that I had expected to result. There was on his side almost a kind of hostility. He remained modest and humble with me, but that made it all the easier to sense his true feelings. He seemed to think I had damaged both him and his cause, and that my belief that I had helped him, or might have helped him, was at best foolishness and more likely arrogance or duplicity. Above all, he would often point out that his opponents thus far had either not shown their opposition, or else done so only in person, or verbally, whereas I had deemed it necessary to have my objections committed to print. Moreover, the few opponents who had delved into the subject, however superficially, had all paid regard to his, the teacher's, point of view, before going on to express their own, whereas I had drawn conclusions from unsystematically collected and partly misunderstood results, which, even if they were broadly correct, were still bound to come over as unconvincing, both to the general public and to experts. And this when the least shimmer of implausibility was the very worst thing that could happen.

It would have been an easy matter for me to dismiss these veiled critiques—after all, his own work represented the height of implausibility—less easy to oppose his continuing distrust, and this constituted the reason I exercised such restraint in my dealings with him. It was his secret conviction that my aim was to cheat him of the renown of being the first person to go public on the mole. Now there was no renown for him personally, just an element of ridicule, and among an ever smaller circle of people at that, for which I certainly had no intention of challenging him. Moreover, in the Foreword to my piece, I had explicitly stated that the teacher was to be accounted for all time the first discoverer of the mole—which wasn't true, he hadn't really "discovered" the mole at all—and the only thing that had prompted me to write at all was feeling for what had happened to him. "The single *raison d'être* of this work"—oh, the pathos, but such was my mood at the time—"is to help the teacher's monograph find the audience it deserves. If it succeeds, then let my name, which is only involved here fortuitously and fleetingly, disappear from the record now and forevermore." I was positively refusing any larger role in the matter; it was almost as though I had sensed the teacher's incredible reproachfulness in advance.

And even so, it was here that he found his point of entry against me, nor do I deny that there was an apparent sense of justification in what he said, or rather hinted, as indeed it was to strike me a few times that he showed greater acuity in his dealings with me than in his work. He claimed my Foreword was duplicitous. If my sole intention was truly to help circulate his writing, then why did I not busy myself with him and his writing to the exclusion of everything else, why did I not show its advantages, its cogency, why did I not limit myself to stressing the importance of the discovery, why on the contrary did I insist on inserting myself into the discovery, all the while completely ignoring his work? Hadn't it been written and published, after all? What was there left to do? If I really thought I had to repeat the discovery, why then did I so solemnly forswear any claims to doing so in my Foreword? It might have been mere false modesty, but in actual fact it was something worse. I was devaluing his discovery; I was drawing attention to it purely in order to devalue it. I had looked into it and then set it aside; things might indeed have grown rather quiet around the discovery, then I came along and started making some noise, but that had the effect of making the teacher's position more difficult than ever. What did the teacher care about the defense of his honor? It was the matter, the matter itself that exercised him. And I was betraying the cause, because I didn't understand it, because I didn't see it straight, because I had no feeling for it. It towered over my tiny comprehension.

He sat in front of me, staring at me with his old rumpled face, and yet this was just his opinion. It wasn't quite right, by the way, that he was only interested in the facts of the case. He was actually quite ambitious and hoped to make some money, which in view of his large family was easy to understand, and yet my interest in the thing seemed comparatively so slight that he thought he could put himself across as perfectly selfless without deviating too far from the truth. And it wasn't even enough for my own inner satisfaction if I told myself that the man's reproaches were basically due to the fact that he was, so to speak, holding onto his mole with two hands, and anyone who approached him with so much as a single upraised finger was bound to strike him as a traitor. That wasn't the case, his behavior was not caused by greed, or at least not greed alone; it was more the irritation that his great efforts and their total lack of success had caused in him. But then his irritability alone didn't explain everything either. Perhaps my interest in the affair really was too slight. A lack of interest on the part of strangers had long since ceased to surprise the teacher: he suffered from it in general, but no longer in particular, whereas here someone had turned up at last who was willing to go into the whole thing in an un-usual way—and then even he didn't understand it. Once the argument was couched in those terms, I couldn't find it in myself to deny it. It's true, I am no zoologist, perhaps if I had discovered the creature then I might have been stirred to the bottom of my heart, but the fact was I hadn't discovered it either. Such an enormous mole is surely a singular creature, but it's wrong to claim the ongoing attention of the whole world for it, especially when the existence of the mole cannot be incontrovertibly established, and it's not possible to pro-duce the creature as evidence. I had to admit, too, that even if I had been the discoverer of the mole, I would probably not have devoted myself to it to the degree the teacher so freely and willingly did.

Now the rift between the teacher and myself would have quickly been smoothed over if my publication had enjoyed success. Alas, it didn't. Perhaps it wasn't well written or per-suasive; commerce is my field and the composition of such a paper probably exceeded my gifts more than was the case with the teacher, even though in point of knowledge I was miles ahead of him. The failure of my paper can be explained in another way too: the timing of its appearance was perhaps unfavorable. The discovery of the mole, incompletely estab-lished at the time, was on the one hand not so remote as to have been forgotten, so that my paper might have had sur-prise on its side; on the other, sufficient time had passed to exhaust such slight interest as there had once been. People who took cognizance of my paper told one another with a kind of dismalness that had characterized the discussion for some years that these futile efforts in this arid matter were getting going again, and some even went so far as to confuse my work with the teacher's.

A leading agricultural journal published the following note, luckily toward the end of the issue in question, and in small print: "The paper on the giant mole has been re-submitted to us. We remember how we laughed heartily at its first appearance years ago. The intervening time has not made it cleverer or ourselves more foolish. Only, we are unable to laugh at it a second time. So let us put the question to our teachers' associations: has a village school-teacher no more pressing task than to go chasing after giant moles?" An unpardonable confusion! They had read neither the first nor the second paper, and the two terms they did manage to glean, "giant mole" and "village schoolteacher" were enough for the gentlemen to take sides in the predict-able way. Various types of recourse suggested themselves, but want of communication with the teacher kept me from pursuing any of them. Rather, I tried to keep the publication secret for as long as possible. But he very quickly got wind of it, as I understood from a remark in a letter from him an-nouncing a visit to me during the Christmas holidays. He wrote: "It's a wicked world, and you're making it easier for it," which was his way of saying that I formed part of it, and wasn't content with my own inborn wickedness either, but was set on making things easier for the world, i.e. I was engaged in supporting a more general badness and helping it to triumph.

Now I had already taken the necessary decisions, I could calmly await his visit and calmly watch him draw up, greet me a little less politely than he liked to do, sit down mutely opposite me, carefully draw out the periodical from the breast pocket of his strangely wadded looking jacket, and push it across to me, open at the place. "I know, I've seen it," I said, pushing the periodical back to him unread. "You've seen it," he said with a sigh—he had the old teacher's habit of repeating answers to questions. "Of course I won't take this lying down," he carried on, rapping on the periodical with a finger and looking at me sharply, as though I disagreed with him; he probably had some clue as to what I might have wanted to say; also I was aware, not so much from his words as from other signs he gave, that he often had a very accurate sense of my intentions, but didn't yield to it and allowed himself to be distracted.

I can repeat what I said to him then almost verbatim, since I made a note of it immediately after our conversation. "You can do as you like," I said, "as of today we will go our separate ways. I think this will neither surprise nor upset you. The note in the paper has not precipitated my decision, merely cemented it. The actual cause lies in the fact that I originally believed my appearance on the scene would assist you, whereas I am now forced to see that I have harmed you in every possible way. I can't say why this has happened, factors governing success and failure are always complex, but you should avoid looking merely for those that seem to implicate me. Remember, you, too, set out with the best of intentions and when you look at the thing as a whole, you failed. Nor am I speaking in jest; it's against myself after all, when I say that the connection with me is just another one of your failures. If I decide to withdraw from the affair now, it's neither cowardice nor betrayal. It even takes a certain amount of resolve; my respect for your person is evident in what I have written, in a sense you have become my teacher too, and the mole is almost dear to me. And yet I will step aside. You are the discoverer and, try as I might, I still seem to get in the way of your possible fame, while I draw failure and pass it onto you. At least that's your view. Enough. The only contrition I can take upon myself is to ask your forgiveness and if you so desire, the admission I've made to you here, repeated in public, for instance in this very magazine."

That was what I said, my words were not wholly ingenuous, but there was ingenuousness very obviously in them. The effect on him was more or less what I had imagined. Most older people have something deceptive or mendacious in their dealings with younger people; that is, you can live among them easily enough, think you get along, know their views on things, receive regular assurances of good feeling, think everything is as it appears to be, and then suddenly, when something dramatic happens and the long-established peace is supposed to swing into effect, these old people get up like strangers and it turns out they hold deeper and stronger views than you thought, they unfurl their banner, so to speak, and only now do you read with alarm what is written on it. The alarm stems particularly from the fact that what the old people are now saying is much more justified, and sensible, as if there were some heightening of the natural modus that was even more natural. The claim they make, unsurpassable in its mendaciousness, is that they were basically always saying what they are saying now, and that it was somehow never possible to sense it amid the generalities.

I must have tunneled a long way into the village schoolteacher because what he did now did not completely surprise me. "My boy," he said, laying his hand over mine, and patting it gently, "I wonder how you ever thought of getting involved in this matter in the first place. The very first time I came across your name I mentioned you to my wife." He moved away from the table, spread his arms and looked at the floor, as though the tiny figure of his wife were standing there for him to talk to. "'For so many years,' I said to her,

'we've been fighting on our own, but now in the city a powerful supporter seems to be entering the lists on our side, a
city businessman by the name of such and such. Is that not
cause for rejoicing? A businessman in the city, that means
something. If it was some old farmer who believed in us and
got up to say so, that wouldn't do much for us, because what
a farmer does is always improper, whether he says that old
village schoolmaster is right, you know, or if he spits rudely
when he hears of us—both have the same effect. And if it
wasn't one farmer, but ten thousand farmers, then the effect
would be, if anything, worse. But a businessman in the city,
that's something else, a man like that will have connections,
even casual remarks of his will make the rounds, new supporters will join him; one person says you can learn from
village schoolteachers, and the following day a lot of people
that from the look of them you would never expect will be
saying it to each other in whispers. Then money starts to
flow; one man starts a collection and others contribute, they
are saying the village schoolteacher needs to be got out of his
village. People turn up, they're not bothered about what he
looks like, they take him into their midst, and since there's
a wife and children as well, they get taken along too. Have
you ever seen city people in action? They're like little birds.
If there's a line of them, they will twitter from right to left
and back again and on and on. And so they lift us twittering
into their coach; there's barely time to nod to all of them
individually. The gentleman on the box adjusts his pince-
nez, swings his whip, and we're off. Everyone waves to the
village as if we were still in it, and not sitting in their midst.
From the city some coaches with especially impatient individuals have set out to meet us. At our approach, they get up
off their seats and crane their necks to see us. The one who

has collected money is in charge, and he tells everyone to re-main calm. By the time we enter the city there's a great line of coaches waiting. We had thought the welcome was over, but at the inn it's only just beginning. In the city, a call is enough to bring a great many people together. The thing that interests the one will interest his neighbor as well. They breathe the same air and inhale the same opinions. Not all the people were able to ride out in carriages, and they're waiting outside the inn. Others might have done so, but for reasons of prestige chose not to. They, too, are waiting now. It's amazing how the man who collected the money is able to keep an eye on everyone.'"

I had been listening to him quietly. The longer he went on, the quieter I became. On the table I had my pamphlet; I had bought up all the available copies. There were only a very few missing, because I had sent out a circular letter asking for all the copies I'd sent out to be returned to me, and most of them had indeed come back. From many people I received very polite letters, to the effect that they didn't recall having been sent such a thing ever, and that if they had, then most regrettably it had been lost. That was fine too, I had noth-ing against that. Only one person asked me to be allowed to keep my pamphlet as a curio and in the spirit of my circu-lar promised not to show it to anyone for the next twenty years. The village schoolmaster hadn't seen this circular let-ter of mine, and I was happy that his words made it so easy for me to show it to him. Moreover, I could do so without the least anxiety because I had taken particular care with its composition, and kept my eye on the interest of the village schoolteacher and his cause at all times. The principal sen-tences ran as follows: "I am not asking for the return of my work because the opinions represented therein are no longer mine, or that I see them as erroneous or even unsusceptible of proof. No, the sole reasons for my request are personal, though very compelling. My view of the substance may not be inferred to any degree, I would like to stress this, and if appropriate, pass it on."

For the moment I kept this letter out of sight, and said: "Are you complaining that these things have failed to come to pass? Why would you do that? Let's not part in any spirit of bitterness. And please try and see that, while you have made a discovery, this discovery does not tower over everything else, and therefore the injustice done to you is not an injustice that towers over all others either. I am not familiar with the regulations of learned societies, but I don't believe that even in an ideal case you would have been afforded a welcome that would have come close to what you outlined to your poor wife. If I hoped for anything from my pamphlet, then it was perhaps that some professor might have been alerted to the case, and that he would have got one of his young students to pursue the matter, that this student might have gone out to see you and would have checked through your and my investigations again in his own way, and that finally, if the result struck him as even worth mentioning—I should say at this point that students are renowned sceptics—then he might have put out a paper of his own in which what you described might have been given a scientific foundation. But even if such a hope had been realized, it still wouldn't have meant much. A paper by a student on such a striking theme might itself have become an object of ridicule. You can see by the example of the agricultural journal how easy it is, and in that regard scientific publications are much more ruthless. Which is understandable, seeing as professors have such vast responsibilities—to science, to posterity—that they can hardly hurl themselves at every new sighting. In that regard, the rest of us have the advantage over them. But I will go on and just assume for now that the student's paper had made its way. What would have happened then? Your name might have appeared a few times, it might have done something for your profession, people would have said: 'Our village schoolmasters are re-nowned for their keensightedness,' and the magazine here, if magazines have such a thing as a memory or a conscience, would have had to issue a public apology, and then a helpful professor would have come forward to secure a scholarship for you. It's a real possibility that efforts might have been made to draw you into the city, perhaps find you a job in a city elementary school and thus given you a chance to avail yourself of the supports that a city offers to your scientific training. If I am to be brutally honest, though, I must say they might not have got beyond the attempt. You would have been summoned here, and you would have come, too, as a supplicant among a hundred others, with no sort of fes-tive welcome. They would have spoken to you, recognized your earnest endeavor, but would have seen that you are an old man, that to embark on a scientific study is a non-sense at such an age, and that you came to your discovery accidentally rather than deliberately, and have no particu-lar plans to pursue it beyond that single case. So they would have ended up leaving you back in your village. Your discov-ery admittedly would have been taken forward because it's not so small that once brought to attention it could ever be wholly lost from sight. But you wouldn't have heard much more about it, and what you would have heard you would barely have been capable of understanding. Every discovery is straightaway incorporated into the body of science and then in a sense stops being a discovery, it is dissolved in the totality and disappears; it takes a scientifically trained eye to even recognize it. It is immediately attached to principles we haven't even heard of, and in the course of scientific disputes, launched into the ether on these same principles. How could we understand? When we listen to such a debate, we may think it's a matter of the discovery, but in fact it's about something completely different."

"Very well," said the village schoolmaster, taking out his pipe and starting to fill it with the tobacco he carried loose in all his pockets, "so you freely undertook an ungrateful task, and are now just as freely resigning from it. Everything is in order." "I'm not pigheaded," I said. "Do you object to anything in my suggestion?" "No, not at all," said the village schoolmaster, and his pipe was already billowing smoke. Not being able to stomach the smell of his tobacco, I got up and started to pace about the room. From our earlier meetings I was used to the fact that the village schoolmaster tended to be rather taciturn with me, and yet, once he had come, wouldn't leave my room. Sometimes it had antagonized me—he wants something from me, I would always think, and offered him money, which he regularly accepted. But he still never left until he was good and ready. Usually his pipe was smoked by then; he stepped around the back of his chair, which he pushed tidily and respectfully up to the table, reached for his walking stick in the corner, eagerly took my hand, and left. Today, though, his silence simply irritated me. If you have offered someone goodbye in an ultimate form as I had, and this meets with the other's agreement, then you get through the rest of what needs to be got through between you as quickly as possible, and don't burden the other with your mute presence to no good end.

Whereas if you looked at the tough old man from behind, the way he was sitting at my table, you might have thought it would be quite impossible to get him out of the room at all.

A Young and Ambitious Student...

A young and ambitious student, who had taken a great interest in the Elberfeld horses* and had diligently read and thought about everything that had been published on the subject, decided spontaneously to conduct his own experiments in that line, and to do so, moreover, in a wholly different, and as he thought, incomparably more correct way than his predecessors. Alas, his financial means were insufficient for him to conduct his experiments on any grand scale, and if the first horse he bought turned out to be mulish, which is something that can only be ascertained after two weeks of the most solid work, then that would have meant the end of his investigations for quite some time. But, because he backed his methods to cope with any degree of mulishness, he wasn't unduly deterred. At any rate, as accorded with his cautious nature, he proceeded methodically to calculate his expenses and the means he would be able to raise. He concluded he would be unable to do without the sum that

* In June 1914, Maurice Maeterlinck published a long essay called "The Thinking Horses of Elberfeld," about the then widely reported efforts of one Karl Krall to train animals in quasi-human thinking and feeling.

his parents—poor tradespeople in the provinces—sent him regularly every month to defray his living expenses, even though of course he would certainly have to give up his studies, which his parents were anxiously following from a distance, if he was to have any hope of the expected success in this new chosen field he was about to enter. That they would have any understanding for this work, or willingly support him in it was out of the question, so, difficult as it was for him, he would have to keep quiet about his intentions and leave his parents thinking he was pursuing his studies as before.

This act of deception was only one of the sacrifices he was prepared to accept in the interests of the cause. To defray the costs that would be involved in his project (expected to be considerable), his allowance from them would not be enough. Henceforth, then, the student decided to devote the greater part of his day, which thus far had been for his studies, to the giving of private lessons. The greater part of the night, meanwhile, would be devoted to his new work. It was not merely because he was compelled to it by financial exigencies that the student lit on the nighttime for the training of his horse: the new principles he hoped to introduce pointed him for various reasons to the night. In his view, the merest break in the animal's concentration would do irreparable damage to the project, and at night he could be reasonably safe from such a thing. The sensitivity that comes over man and beast both waking and working at night was an integral feature of his plan. Unlike other experts, he had no fear of the wildness of the animal, he positively encouraged it—yes, he sought to produce it, not through the whip admittedly, but by the irritant of his constant presence and constant teaching.

He claimed that in the correct training of a horse there must be no incremental progress; incremental progress, for which various trainers had claimed such absurdly excessive credit of late, was nothing but a figment of the trainers' imagination, or else—and this was actually worse—the clearest possible sign that there would never be any overall advance. He himself swore to avoid nothing so strenuously as incremental progress. The modesty of his predecessors in thinking they had achieved something with the teaching of pretty arithmetical tricks was incomprehensible to him. It was as if you wanted to make it your end in the education of children, to teach the child nothing but multiplication tables, no matter if the child was deaf, blind, and insentient to the world beyond. All that was so foolish, and the mistakes of the other trainers sometimes struck him as so revoltingly obvious, that he would end up almost doubting himself, because it was surely impossible that a single person, and an inexperienced one at that, albeit driven by a deep and positively wild, though still untested conviction, could be right in the teeth of all the experts.

Blumfeld, an Elderly Bachelor...

Blumfeld, an elderly bachelor, was one evening climbing up to his flat, which was a laborious process, because he lived up on the sixth floor. As he climbed the stairs, he thought to himself, as he had quite often lately, that this completely solitary life was burdensome indeed, the fact that he had to slink up these six flights of stairs to arrive in his empty room, there, secretly still, to slip into his dressing gown, light his pipe, and browse a little in an issue of the French magazine he had subscribed to for several years now, while sipping at a cherry brandy of his own manufacture, and finally, after half an hour of this, to go to bed, which, to make matters worse, he had to comprehensively remake, because the cleaner, impervious to instruction, always left it any old how. Some companion, some spectator at these activities, would have been very welcome to Blumfeld. He had already wondered about the possibility of acquiring a little dog. Such an animal is diverting and, above all, loyal and grateful; one of Blumfeld's colleagues had such an animal, he refuses to go with anyone but his master, and if he hasn't seen him for a few moments, he welcomes him with loud barking, clearly an expression of joy at having refound his extraordinary benefactor and master. Admittedly, a dog has his drawbacks too. However tidy you try and keep him, he'll dirty your room. It's impossible to avoid, you can hardly give him a bath in hot water before letting him in each time, that would undermine his constitution. But a dirty room is something Blumfeld can't abide, the cleanliness of his room is indispensable to him, several times a week he has it out with the unfortunately not so scrupulous cleaner. Since she's hard of hearing, he conducts her to those parts of the room whose cleanliness leaves something to be desired. Through such severity, he has secured a state of affairs where the condition of the room more or less accords with his wishes. Introducing a dog into it would be tantamount to inviting the dirt, so effortfully excluded, back into his room. Fleas, the constant companions of dogs, would appear. Then, once there were fleas, could the moment be far off when Blumfeld would have to leave his cosy room to the dog and go and live somewhere else? And dirt was only one drawback. Dogs get sick and who really understands animal diseases? Then you would have the animal crouched in a corner or limping around, whimpering, coughing or choking on some pain or other, you wrap him up in a blanket, whistle a tune to him, push a saucer of milk in front of him; in short, you look after him in the hope that, as is indeed possible, it's a passing sickness, but it may turn out instead to be something seriously disgusting and infectious. And even if the dog stays healthy, he will one day grow old; you might not be able to decide in time to give the faithful animal away and so the moment comes when it's your own life that's looking back at you from those weeping dog's eyes. Then you're saddled with a half-blind, wheezing animal, so corpulent it can hardly move, and then the pleasures the dog afforded you back in the day are dearly bought indeed. However much Blumfeld would like a dog just at the moment, he would rather trudge up the stairs alone for another thirty years than be discommoded by an old dog like that later, who, groaning even louder than his master, drags himself from step to step.

So Blumfeld will remain alone. He doesn't have the physical yearnings of an old spinster, who craves some inferior being around her, for her to protect, on which she can exercise her tenderness, which she will constantly pamper, for which purposes a cat or a canary or even a few goldfish might do. And if she can't have any of those, then she'll make do with a flowerbox outside the window. Blumfeld, however, is out for a companion, an animal that doesn't require much in the way of maintenance, that won't mind the occasional kick, that will survive a night on the street, but that, should Blumfeld require it, will be on the spot with barking, leaping, and licking of hands. That's what Blumfeld is in the market for, but since, as he concedes, he can't have it without considerable drawbacks, then he declines; though, in accordance with his methodical nature, he can't but return to the idea from time to time, as for instance, this evening.

Standing outside the door, and reaching into his pocket for his key, he is struck by a sound coming from inside. A strange clattering sound, but lively and above all regular. Since Blumfeld has just been thinking about dogs, he is put in mind of the sound of paws on parquet floors. But paws don't clatter, so these aren't paws. He hurriedly unlocks the door and turns on the electric light. He isn't prepared for what meets his eye. As if by magic, two little blue and white striped celluloid balls are bouncing side by side on the floor; when the one hits the ground, the other is in midair, and they play tirelessly together. At school once, Blumfeld saw little balls bouncing like this in the course of an experiment with electricity, but these balls are pretty large, and are jumping freely around the room, and of course there is no electrical experiment. Blumfeld bends down to get a closer look at them. There is no doubt about it, they are ordinary balls, probably they contain some smaller balls within them, and they are what is producing the clattering sound. Blumfeld waves his hands to check that they aren't secured to some sort of string or something, but no, their movement is perfectly independent. Too bad that Blumfeld isn't a small boy, two balls like that would have been a wonderful surprise, whereas now the whole thing makes a faintly disagreeable impression on him. It's not the worst thing, really, to be an obscure bachelor and lead an invisible life; now someone, never mind who, has found him out, and sent him those two strange balls.

He tries to grab one of them, but they retreat from him, drawing him further into the room. "How undignified," he thinks, "to be chasing after a couple of balls," but then he stops and watches as, once his pursuit has slackened off, they stay in the same place. "I will try and catch them anyway," he thinks, and sets off after them. They straightaway flee, but a splayfooted Blumfeld shepherds them into a corner of the room, and in front of a trunk that's standing there, he manages to catch one of the balls. The ball is small and cool to the touch, and spins in his hand, evidently trying to escape. And the other ball too, as though seeing the predicament of its fellow, starts jumping higher than before and jumps so high that it strikes Blumfeld's hand. It strikes the hand, jumping up rapidly, changes its line of attack, then, unable to do anything to the hand that's enclosing the ball, it jumps higher still, probably in an effort to reach Blumfeld's face. Blumfeld could catch this ball too, and lock them both away, but just at that moment it strikes him as undignified to take such measures against two little balls. It's fun too, isn't it, to own two little balls; they'll tire soon enough, roll under a cupboard somewhere, and keep shtum. In spite of his thought, Blumfeld, in an access of something like rage, flings the ball to the ground; it's a wonder the thin, almost transparent veneer of celluloid doesn't shatter. Without a second's pause, the two balls resume their previous pattern of low, alternating bounces.

Blumfeld calmly gets undressed, tidies his clothes away in the wardrobe—he usually likes to check the cleaner has left everything there in good order. Once or twice he looks over his shoulder at the balls—since he has given up pursuing them, they seem to be following him—they have moved closer and are bouncing just behind him. Blumfeld pulls on his dressing gown, and then crosses the room to fetch a pipe from the rack there. Involuntarily, before turning round, he kicks out a heel, but the balls succeed in staying out of the way and are not struck. As he goes for his pipe now, the balls join him right away. He shuffles along in his slippers, taking irregular steps, but almost without a break the balls follow him step by step. Blumfeld turns round suddenly— he wants to see how the balls cope with that. But no sooner has he turned than the balls move through a semicircle, and are once again behind him; this happens each time he turns. Like junior members of a retinue, they seek to avoid parading in front of Blumfeld. Thus far, the only reason they did so was to introduce themselves to him, but now they have entered his service.

Up to this point, Blumfeld's recourse on finding himself in exceptional situations that could not be mastered by sheer strength was to pretend he hadn't noticed anything amiss. Often it helped; at least it improved his position. This is what he does again now, standing with a thoughtful pout in front of his pipe rack, selecting a pipe, filling it with unusual thoroughness from the tobacco pouch also there, and just letting the balls bounce away to their hearts' content behind him. Only he is reluctant to go to the table, he feels something akin to pain at the thought of their bouncing in time to his footfall. So he stands there, spending an unnecessarily long time filling his pipe, and gauging the distance between his position and the table. At last, he overcomes his weakness and covers the distance with such loud stamps of his feet that he doesn't even hear the balls. When he is sitting down, admittedly, there they are, bouncing behind his armchair just as audibly as before.

Within reach across the table by the wall is a shelf where the bottle of cherry brandy is kept, ringed by little glasses. Next to it is the stack of French periodicals. But instead of getting everything he needs, Blumfeld sits there quite still and stares into his unlit pipe bowl. He is on the alert, very abruptly his rigidity vanishes, and with a jerk he turns around in the armchair. But the balls are every bit as alert. Or else they unthinkingly follow the rule that governs their existence. At the moment Blumfeld turns, they too change their location and hide behind his back. Now Blumfeld is sitting with his back to the table, the cold pipe in his hand. The balls are now bouncing under the table, and because there's a rug there, they are correspondingly quiet. This is much better; there are only weak dull sounds, you have to concentrate hard to even hear them. Blumfeld admittedly *is* concentrating hard, and he hears them all too well. But that's just how it is now, probably in a little while he won't hear them at all. The fact that they get so little change out of carpets strikes Blumfeld as a grave weakness in the balls.

All you need do is push a rug or two under them, and they are almost powerless. Admittedly, only for a certain time, and moreover their mere being seems to constitute a sort of power in itself.

Now Blumfeld really could use a dog, a healthy young animal that would make short work of those balls; he pictures the dog swiping at them with its paws, driving them away from their position; he chases them all round the room, and in the end gets them between his jaws. Yes, it's quite possible that Blumfeld will be acquiring a dog shortly.

But for the time being it's only Blumfeld that the balls have to beware of, and he doesn't feel like destroying them either, perhaps he lacks the resolve for that. He generally gets home in the evening tired out from work and now, just when he needs quiet, there is this surprise waiting for him. He starts to feel just how tired he is. He will destroy the balls, no question, and sooner rather than later, but not right away and probably not until tomorrow. If he were being dispassionate, he would have to say the balls are behaving pretty modestly. For instance they could be jumping out from time to time, showing themselves, and then go back to their place, or they could jump higher, to strike the underside of the table, thus making up for the muffling effect of the carpet. But they don't do either thing; they don't want to provoke Blumfeld needlessly, evidently they're limiting themselves to the bare essentials.

These essentials, admittedly, are enough to make Blumfeld feel ill at ease at his table. He has been sitting there for a few minutes, and already he's thinking of going to bed. One of his reasons is that he is unable to smoke where he is, having forgotten his matches on the bedside table. So he would have to fetch them, and once he's there, it's probably better just to stay there and lie down. He has an ulterior thought, namely that the balls in their blind need to always be behind him, will jump up onto the bed, and then, intentionally or otherwise, he can easily crush them. The possible objection that the remnants of the balls might be able to jump too, he rejects. Even the extraordinary has its limits. Ordinary balls bounce as well, though not incessantly; fragments of balls never do, and they won't in this case either.

"Hup!" he calls out, almost emboldened by the thought, and tramps off to bed with the balls following him. His hopes seem to be borne out; as he stands deliberately right beside the bed, one of the balls promptly jumps up onto it. Then something unexpected happens, namely the other ball goes underneath it. Blumfeld had not considered the possibility that the balls could bounce underneath the bed. He is a little dismayed by this one ball, even though he feels it unfair of him, because by bouncing underneath the bed, this ball is perhaps discharging its duty even better than its fellow on the bed. Now it's a question of where the balls decide to go, because Blumfeld doesn't believe they are capable of operating separately for long. And in fact, a moment later, the lower ball now jumps up onto the bed. "Now I've got them!" thinks Blumfeld, hot with joy, and he tears off his dressing gown to throw himself into his bed. But just then, that same ball jumps back under the bed. Excessively disappointed, Blumfeld slumps back. The ball probably just took a look at conditions on the bed and found it didn't care for them. And, of course, now the other ball follows suit, and of course it stays under the bed, because under is better. "Now I'm going to be stuck with those two drummers all night," thinks Blumfeld, biting his lip and shaking his head.

He feels sad, though he doesn't know what the balls could

do to harm him at night. His sleep is extremely sound; he will easily manage to ignore their slight noise. To be sure of this, as experience has already taught him, he pushes a couple of rugs under the bed. It's as though he had a small dog there, and wanted to make sure it's comfortable; and as though the balls were getting tired and sleepy too, their jumps becoming lower and slower than up until now. As Blumfeld kneels down by the bedside and shines a flashlight under the bed, he sometimes has a sense that the balls will stay forever on the carpets, that's how feebly they're falling, how slowly they're rolling a few inches this way or that. Then, admittedly, they get a grip on themselves and perform. Still, Blumfeld thinks it perfectly possible that when he looks under the bed in the morning, he will find just two harmless and motionless toys.

But they don't seem to be able to keep bouncing until the morning, because no sooner is Blumfeld lying in bed than he can't hear them anymore. He strains to pick up a sound, leans right out of his bed—nothing at all. It's not possible for that all to be because of the rugs; no, the only explanation is that the balls have stopped jumping. Either they can't lift themselves off the soft rugs and have for the moment given up, or—and this strikes Blumfeld as the likelier of the two—they will never jump again. Blumfeld could of course get up and check, but in his satisfaction that quiet has returned, he remains lying where he is, he won't even send a look the way of those pacified balls. He doesn't even miss his evening smoke; he rolls over onto his side and is asleep immediately.

But he is not undisturbed; his sleep is dreamless, as it always is, just very restless. Innumerable times he is woken by the fancy that someone is knocking on his door. Of course he knows there is no one; who could possibly come knocking on his lonely bachelor's door at night. Even though he knows it, he still can't help leaping up and looking tensely in the direction of the door, his mouth agape, his eyes starting, strands of hair shaking on his damp brow. He tries to keep count of the number of times he is woken, but driven demented by the vast numbers that come up, he falls back to sleep. He thinks he has an idea where the knocking is coming from, it's not the door at all, but somewhere else, yet in the muzziness of sleep he can't remember what this assumption of his is grounded on. All he knows is that many tiny disgusting little taps, put together, make a big powerful knock. He thinks he would tolerate all the disgustingness of the little taps if he could avoid the knocks, but for some reason it's too late, he is unable to intervene, he's missed his moment, he doesn't even have words, his mouth opens only for a mute yawn and, in fury, he mashes his face down in the pillow. This is his night.

In the morning he is woken by the knocking of the cleaner and with a sigh of relief he greets her gentle knocking—it always annoyed him that it was inaudible. And he is on the point of calling out "Come in" when he hears another lively knocking, still muted, but positively warlike. It is the balls under the bed. Have they woken up—have they, unlike him, gathered fresh strength over night? "One moment," Blumfeld calls to the charlady, jumps out of bed, but taking care to keep his back to the balls, throws himself to the floor with his back to them, then twists his head in the direction of the balls—and—he almost swears. Like children pushing their unwanted blankets away, the balls, presumably through a sequence of nudgings kept up all night, the balls have managed to push the rugs so far under the bed that they have gained access to the parquet floor and are able to make a noise. "Get back on the rug!" says Blumfeld with an angry expression. When the balls are quiet again, thanks to the rugs, he calls the charlady in. While she, a fat, obtuse woman with a stiff upright gait, sets out his breakfast on the table and does a few other essential things, Blumfeld stands motionless in his dressing gown beside his bed to keep the balls in place. He watches her to check whether she has noticed anything. Hard of hearing as she is, it's very unlikely, and Blumfeld puts it down to irritability brought on by his bad night's sleep when he thinks he sees her stop from time to time, grab hold of some piece of furniture, and listen with raised eyebrows. He wishes she would get a move on, but if anything she's even slower than usual. Clumsily she loads herself up with Blumfeld's clothes and boots, and goes out into the corridor with them. She stays gone a long time and there are very occasional thumps as she brushes them. And all this time Blumfeld has to wait by the bed, unable to move, so as not to bring the balls out behind him; has to let his coffee (which he likes to drink hot) go cold, and do nothing but stare at the drawn curtains, behind which the new day is murkily brightening. Finally the charlady is finished, bids him a good morning, and is on her way out. But before she finally takes her leave, she stops by the door muttering and giving Blumfeld a long stare. Blumfeld is on the point of asking her a question when she finally goes. He feels like yanking the door open and yelling at her for being such a stupid old woman. But when he thinks about what he actually has against her, he sees only the contradiction that she certainly hasn't noticed anything but wanted to give the impression that she had. Such bewildering thoughts he has! And after only one single bad night's sleep! He finds a little explanation for this in the departure from his habits—he didn't smoke or drink. "If I ever," is the conclusion of his thinking, "don't smoke and don't drink, I know I'm in for a bad night."

From now on he means to pay more attention to his physical well-being, and to make a start he takes the cotton wool from the home pharmacy kit which hangs over the bedside table and shoves two cotton-wool balls in his ears. Then he gets up and takes a trial step. The balls set off after him, but he almost can't hear them, and a little more cotton wool is enough to render them completely inaudible. Blumfeld executes a few more steps: there is no particular unpleasantness. Each party is on its own, Blumfeld and the balls, they are connected to each other, but they don't interfere with each other. Only when Blumfeld happens to turn round a little quickly and one of the balls doesn't get out of his way in time, he strikes it with his knee. That's the only incident to report, otherwise Blumfeld drinks his coffee in peace—he is ravenously hungry, it's as though he hadn't slept at all, but had been on a long walk—washes in cold, incredibly refreshing water, and gets dressed. Up until now, he hasn't drawn the curtains, having taken the road of caution and preferring to remain in the half dark; he doesn't need any snoops to watch him and the balls. But now that he's ready to go, he needs to make arrangements for the balls in case—though he doesn't think it likely—they should try to follow him out onto the street. At this point he has a good idea. He opens the large wardrobe and stands there with his back to it. It's as though they could read his intentions, because they avoid the inside of the wardrobe and use every bit of available space between Blumfeld and the wardrobe, jumping momentarily, if nothing else is possible, inside the wardrobe, but then coming speeding out of its darkness. It seems it's not possible to drive them any further inside; they would rather violate their duty and stand laterally to Blumfeld. But their little cunning is unavailing, because now Blumfeld backs right into the wardrobe, and they are compelled to follow him. And with that their fate is sealed, because the floor of the wardrobe is littered with various little items, such as boots, boxes, little cases, that are all—Blumfeld regrets it now—tidily arranged, but that make things quite a bit harder for the balls. And when Blumfeld now, having almost drawn shut the door of the wardrobe, suddenly, with a leap the likes of which he has not performed for several years, leaves the wardrobe, shuts the door, and turns the key in the lock, the balls are locked away. "So much for you," thinks Blumfeld and wipes the sweat from his face. How the balls racket in the wardrobe! They give every impression of feeling desperate. Blumfeld, on the other hand, is mightily pleased. He leaves his room and even the drabness of the common parts feels like a boon to him. He frees his ears of their cotton wool, and the myriad sounds of the awakening house enchant him. There are few people around; it is still very early.

Downstairs, in the passage outside the low door to the charlady's basement apartment, stands her ten-year-old son. The spit and image of his mother, not one of the old woman's upsetting features has been omitted from the child's countenance. Bandy-legged, his hands in his trouser pockets, he stands there rasping, because he has croup and finds it difficult to breathe. But whereas Blumfeld normally speeds his step when he sees the boy in his path, to keep their encounters to a minimum, today he is moved to almost stop. Even if the boy was born of that woman, and shows every sign of his origins, he is just a child, and that misshapen head is full of childish ideas. If one were to speak to him gently and ask him something, he would probably reply in a treble voice, innocent and respectful, and one might get over one's revulsion in the end and give him a pat on the cheek. So thinks Blumfeld, but walks on by anyway. Once on the street, he notices the weather is milder than it appeared in his room. The overnight fog is dispersing, swept away by a powerful wind, and there are patches of blue in the sky. Blumfeld feels some gratitude to the balls that he is out of his room much earlier than usual; he's even left the newspaper unread on his table. At any rate he has gained a lot of time, and can now afford to walk slowly. It is strange how little the balls concern him since he has parted from them. As long as they were after him, it might have been possible to take them for something belonging to him, something that would influence people's opinion of him, but now they are shut up in the wardrobe, like a toy. And this causes Blumfeld to think that the best way of rendering the balls harmless might be to return them to their original intended function. The boy will still be standing in the landing; Blumfeld will take him the balls, not on any temporary basis but as an outright gift, which will certainly be tantamount to an order for their destruction. And even if they should remain intact, in the hands of the boy they will still amount to less than in his wardrobe; the whole house will watch the boy playing with them, other children will join in, the general view that what is at issue here is some plaything and not Blumfeld's life-companions will harden and finally become irresistible.

Blumfeld runs back inside. The boy has just gone down the cellar steps and is about to open the door. Blumfeld is obliged to call the boy, and use his ridiculous name, ridiculous like everything connected with this boy. He does so. "Alfred," he calls, "er, Alfred." The boy hesitates a long time. "Oh, come along," calls Blumfeld, "I've got something for you." The janitor's two little daughters have come out of the door opposite and take up positions nosily right and left of Blumfeld. They are much quicker on the uptake than the boy, and can't understand why he won't come up straight away. They beckon to him to come, not letting Blumfeld out of sight, but are unable to guess what sort of present is waiting for Alfred. They are consumed with curiosity, shifting from one foot to the other. Blumfeld is amused by them as much as by the boy. The boy seems at last to have made sense of everything in his mind, and begins stiffly and awkwardly to climb up the stairs. Not even in his gait does he diverge from his mother, who chooses this moment to appear in the doorway. Blumfeld calls out with excessive volume, so that the woman will understand and can supervise the putting into effect of his instructions, should it be required. "Up in my room," says Blumfeld, "I have two lovely balls. Would you like them?" The boy just pulls a face, he has no idea what to do. He turns round and looks questioningly at his mother. But the girls right away start to hop around behind Blumfeld, begging him for the balls. "You'll be able to play with them as well," Blumfeld tells them, but he's waiting for a reply from the boy. He could of course just give the balls to the girls, but they strike him as being a little irresponsible and he feels he can trust the boy more. He, in the meantime, has applied to his mother for advice, and without a word having been exchanged between them, now nods in agreement when Blumfeld repeats his question. "Then listen carefully," says Blumfeld, who is perfectly happy not to be thanked for his generosity, "your mother has a key to my room, you'll have to borrow it from her. Here is the key to my wardrobe, and the balls are in the wardrobe. Be sure to lock the wardrobe and the room behind you. But you can do whatever you like with the balls, and you don't need to give them back to me. You got that?" Unfortunately the boy hasn't. Blumfeld wanted to make everything particularly clear to this endlessly dim creature, but as a result he has said everything too many times, brought up the keys to the wardrobe and the room confusingly and too often, and as a result the boy isn't gazing at him as his benefactor, but scowling at him as a tempter. The girls, of course, have straightaway understood everything. They press up against Blumfeld and put out their hands for his key. "Wait," says Blumfeld, getting annoyed about everything. Also time is passing, and he can't hang around here forever. If only the charwoman would say she had understood him and will help the boy as needed. Instead of which she's still standing in the doorway, smirking like someone hard of hearing, and maybe thinking that Blumfeld from upstairs has suddenly come over all soft about her son, and will ask to hear him recite his multiplication table next. For his part, Blumfeld can hardly go down the stairs again and shout his plea into the charwoman's ears, that her son should for the love of God free him of those two balls. He has violated his natural inclinations enough already in leaving the key to his wardrobe in the possession of such a family for a whole day. It's really not to spare himself that he's handing the key to the boy, instead of taking him upstairs and giving him the balls there. He can hardly give the balls to him upstairs and then, as would presumably happen, remove them again right away, by drawing them away with him as his retinue. "So you don't understand me?" asks Blumfeld almost mournfully, after he's girded himself up for a fresh explanation, but then, seeing the vacant gaze of the boy, broken off again immediately. A vacant look like that leaves one helpless. It could lead one to say more than one meant to say, merely in the hope of pouring a little sense into the vacancy.

"What if we get the balls for him," call the girls. They are clever, they have understood that they can only get at the balls by the mediation of the boy, and that they need to help with the mediation. A clock in the janitor's flat strikes and gives Blumfeld a gee-up. "Then you take the key," says Blumfeld, and the key is more taken from him than given by him. The confidence he would have felt if he'd managed to hand the key to the boy would have been incomparably greater. "Get the room key from your mother," Blumfeld manages to add, "and when you come back with the balls, I want you to leave her both the keys." "All right," call the girls, and go spilling down the stairs. They have grasped everything, absolutely everything, and as though Blumfeld was infected by the slow-wittedness of the boy, he is briefly at a loss to know how they managed to follow his explanations so quickly.

Now they are downstairs, tugging at the skirts of the charwoman, but however much he'd like to stay and watch them perform their task, Blumfeld can't, and it's not just because time is going by; it's also because he doesn't want to be present when the balls escape into the open. He would even like to put several streets between them when the girls open the door to his room. There is no knowing what else the balls are capable of. And so for the second time this morning, he steps outside the front door. He just manages to catch the charlady pushing the girls away, and the boy moving his bandy legs to come to her help. Blumfeld doesn't understand how such people as the charwoman manage to prosper in this world and multiply.

On Blumfeld's way to the linen factory where he works, thoughts of work gradually gain the upper hand over everything else. He speeds up his steps and in spite of the delay for which the boy was entirely responsible, he is still the first one in the office. This office is a small room walled with glass: it contains a desk for Blumfeld and two standing desks for a couple of juniors who work under him. Even though these standing desks are as small and narrow as though they'd been designed for schoolchildren, they do make space in the office very tight, and the juniors are unable to sit anywhere, because then there would be no room for Blumfeld to have a chair. So they spend all day pressed against their desks. This is certainly very uncomfortable for them, and it also has the effect of making it harder for Blumfeld to keep an eye on them. Often they press themselves eagerly against their desks, not to work at all, oh no, but to whisper to each other or even to nap. Blumfeld has no end of trouble with them and the support they give him in his gigantic work is anything but adequate. What this work consists of is nothing less than the organization of the entire flow of materials and money to the home-workers from whom the factory buys certain hand-stitched articles. In order to appreciate the scale of this work, one would need to have a minute insight into the totality of all the relationships involved. But, since the death of Blumfeld's immediate superior a few years ago, there is no one who has had such an insight, for which reason Blumfeld cannot concede anyone a right to be the judge of his work. The manager Herr Ottomar, for instance, quite clearly underestimates Blumfeld's work. Of course he acknowledges the credit that Blumfeld has earned in the course of his twenty years at the factory—acknowledging it not merely because he has to, but because he respects Blumfeld as a loyal and trustworthy human being; but he nevertheless underestimates his work because he thinks it could be arranged more simply and thus in every respect more advantageously than the way Blumfeld does it. It is said, and this is not implausible, that the reason Ottomar puts in so few appearances in Blumfeld's department is to spare himself the irritation that the sight of Blumfeld's working methods causes him. Being thus underappreciated is of course sad for Blumfeld, but there is nothing to be done about it; he can hardly compel Ottomar's attendance for a month in his, Blumfeld's, department, in order to study the various tasks requiring to be done there, and apply his own, allegedly superior methods to them, and allowing himself, through the collapse of the department that would be an inevitable consequence of their application, to be persuaded by Blumfeld. Therefore Blumfeld merely goes about his work as he has always done, is alarmed each time Ottomar puts in one of his rare appearances, then with the subordinate's sense of duty makes some feeble attempt to demonstrate this or that facility, whereupon the other, nodding silently, walks on with lowered eyes; and in a way he suffers less from this underestimation than from the thought that when he one day comes to leave his job, the immediate consequence will be a great and insoluble confusion, because he knows no one in the factory who can fill in for him and take over his job in such a way that the most serious blockages could be avoided over a period of several months in the business. And if the boss underestimates someone, then of course the employees merely try and outdo him in this. Therefore everyone underestimates Blumfeld's work; no one thinks it a necessary part of his training to spend any time working in Blumfeld's department, and when employees are taken on, no one is automatically assigned to Blumfeld's section either. The result is that Blumfeld's section is chronically short on young blood. It took weeks of dogged infighting for Blumfeld, who thus far had been assisted merely by a single servant, to claim the assigning of a junior. On an almost daily basis Blumfeld would appear in Ottomar's office and explain to him calmly and in detail why he needed a junior in his section. It wasn't because Blumfeld wanted to take things easy— Blumfeld had no intention of taking things easy, he was working feverishly at his own excessive tasks and had no thought of stopping—but if Herr Ottomar would just think how the business had developed over time, every section had been allowed to grow accordingly, and only his, Blumfeld's, had been overlooked. And yet it was precisely here that the work had increased! At the time when Blumfeld had started, which Herr Ottomar would surely not be able to remember, they had had to deal with about a dozen seamstresses, while today the number was somewhere between fifty and sixty. Such work demands strength. Blumfeld could vouch for the fact that he drove himself to exhaustion at his work, but that he could successfully accomplish it was something he was no longer able to guarantee. Herr Ottomar never turned down Blumfeld's petitions flat, he couldn't do that to an employee of such long standing, but his way of barely listening, for instance talking past the pleading Blumfeld to other employees, giving him half assurances, forgetting them completely in a day or two—that was really pretty offensive. Not so much for Blumfeld, as Blumfeld is no fantasist—Blumfeld is a realist. Honor and appreciation are all very well, but Blumfeld can do without them: in spite of everything he will remain at his post for as long as he humanly can. One thing is certain, he has right on his side, and in the end, though it may take a long time, what is right is sure to prevail. And lo! Blumfeld did eventually get himself assigned a couple of juniors, but what juniors. One might have supposed Ottomar thought he could express his contempt for Blumfeld's section even more clearly than by denying him juniors—by the assigning of them. It was even possible that the only reason Ottomar had for so long put off Blumfeld was because he had been looking for two such juniors, and, not unnaturally, it had taken him a long time to find them. And now Blumfeld could no longer complain, as the reply was all too predictable: he had asked for a junior and been given two; that was how cannily Ottomar had arranged everything. Of course Blumfeld did continue to complain, but only because he was driven to do so by the extremity of his need, not because he had any thought he would find relief. Nor did he complain emphatically, only a little on the side, if there happened to be an opportunity to do so. In spite of that the rumor spread among his ill-intentioned colleagues that someone had asked Ottomar whether it was possible that Blumfeld, who had been given such extraordinary assistance, was still complaining. To which Ottomar had replied, it was true, Blumfeld continued to complain, and with good reason. He, Ottomar, had finally understood, and he intended over time to allow Blumfeld one junior for every seamstress, coming to an eventual total of sixty. And if that turned out to be insufficient, he would send more and would not stop until the madhouse that for some years now was Blumfeld's section was completely full up.

What was striking about this was that Ottomar's general managerial style was well imitated, even though Ottomar himself—of this Blumfeld had no doubt—was far from ever expressing himself in such terms, or anything resembling them, about Blumfeld. The whole thing was an invention on the part of the layabouts in the first-floor offices, and Blumfeld simply ignored it, wishing he could have ignored the presence of his juniors in the same way. But there they stood, and it was impossible to think them away. Weak, pale boys. According to their employment papers, they were past graduation age, though it seemed doubtful to him. You wouldn't even have wanted to entrust them to a schoolteacher, that's how clearly they belonged in the care of their mothers. They could barely even move, and long periods of standing around seemed to take it out of them, especially at the beginning. If you let them out of your sight, they would crumple up with feebleness, standing there skewed or bent over in a corner. Blumfeld tried to point out to them that they would be crippled for life if they always gave in to the dictates of comfort like that. To entrust the juniors with even a small task was risky. Once he had asked one of them to bring him something; it was only a few steps away, but in his overeagerness the fellow had run off and gashed his knee against his desk. The room at the time was full of seamstresses, and the desks full of their wares, but Blumfeld had had to drop everything and take the crying junior back to the office and give him a little bandage. But even this zeal on the part of the juniors was merely for show, as, like children, they sometimes wanted to excel, but much more often, or in fact almost always, they wanted to dupe and deceive their superior. Once, when there was a great deal of work to be done, a sweat-dripping Blumfeld had raced past them and noticed that they were between bales of material, secretly swapping stamps. He felt like cuffing them, it was the only punishment for such behavior, but they were children and Blumfeld couldn't have infanticide on his conscience. And so he went on torturing himself with them. Originally he had imagined that the juniors would help him with the little things that demanded so much concentration and alertness at the time for the distribution of materials. He had pictured himself standing behind his desk at the center of things, keeping everything in view and making the entries in ledgers, while the juniors ran back and forth on his say-so, giving things out as required. He had imagined his vigilance, though sharp indeed, would not be sufficient for such a crowd, and would be supplemented by that of the juniors, and that these juniors would over time garner experience, not depend in every instance on his telling them what to do, and gradually learn by themselves to draw distinctions among the seamstresses with respect to their relative needs and their trustworthiness. But with these juniors any such hopes were misplaced, Blumfeld soon saw that; he should never have encouraged them to talk to the seamstresses in the first place. Some, they had never approached at all, because they were afraid of them or took against them; others to whom they had taken a shine, they would often accompany as far as the door. For these ones they would bring whatever the seamstresses wanted, pressing the items into their hands with a kind of furtiveness—even if it was something the seamstresses were perfectly entitled to—collecting on an empty shelf various bits and bobs for these preferred parties, valueless remnants, often enough, but also usable items, happily beckoning to them from a distance behind Blumfeld's back and getting sweets pushed into their mouth in return. Blumfeld soon put an end to these practices and drove them into a little corner whenever the seamstresses were due. But for a long time they thought that was a great injustice, and they sulked, broke out of their corner—though of course they never dared to raise their heads—banged loudly on the windowpanes to draw the seamstresses' attention to the ill-treatment they had, in their opinion, received at the hands of Blumfeld.

At the same time they are completely oblivious to the wrongs they themselves perpetrate. So, for instance, they are almost always late for work. Blumfeld, their boss, who from his earliest youth took it for granted that he had to arrive at least half an hour before the office opened—it wasn't over-zealousness that drove him to it, not any exaggerated sense of duty, no, just an innate sense of what was required—is usually kept waiting for his juniors for over an hour. Chewing his breakfast roll, he generally stands behind the desk in the room, balancing the accounts in the seamstresses' little logbooks. Before long he is immersed in the work, and there is nothing else on his mind. Then he is suddenly so alarmed that for a while after, the pen shakes in his hands. One junior has charged in, it's as though he is falling over, with one hand he is holding onto himself somewhere, and with the other he is pressing his heaving chest—but all this charade amounts to is that he is offering an apology for his tardiness that is so ridiculous that Blumfeld prefers to disregard it, because if he didn't he would feel obliged to give the boy the thrashing he deserved. As it is, he just glowers at him, then points him with one hand to the pen, and returns to his own work. One might have expected the junior to see the charity of his boss and to hurry to his place of work. Not a bit of it, he doesn't hurry, he takes fairy steps, he walks on tippy-toe; he sets one foot just in front of the other. Is he trying to get a rise out of his boss? No, it's not that either. It's just that same mixture of fear and cheek in the teeth of which one is helpless.

How else account for the fact that today Blumfeld, who has come into work unusually late himself, now, at the end of a long wait—he has lost his taste for balancing the books—through the clouds of dust that the wretched servant has whipped up in the air in front of him, sees the two juniors together on the street, approaching peaceably. They have their arms slung around each other and seem to be saying important things to each other, but they will have little, if anything, to do with work. The nearer they come to the glass door, the more they slow their steps. Finally, one of them is clasping the doorknob, but refrains from turning it. They are still chatting and laughing together. "Show the gentlemen in, why don't you?" Blumfeld calls out to the servant with raised hands. But when the juniors enter, Blumfeld is no longer in any mood to remonstrate; he doesn't reply to their greeting and walks over to his desk. He starts to make some calculations, but looks up from time to time to see what the juniors are up to. One of them seems to be very tired, yawning and rubbing his eyes; once he has hung his jacket up on the nail, he uses the opportunity to lean against the wall for a spell; on the road he was fresh enough, but the proximity to work has made him suddenly tired. The other junior does feel like work, but only work of a certain kind. Thus it has apparently been his desire forever to sweep the floor.

As a line of work, it's not for him: sweeping is a task for the servant; in his heart of hearts Blumfeld has nothing against the junior sweeping—let him sweep if he wants to, it's hardly possible to do it any worse than the servant. But if the junior wants to sweep, then he needs to get in a little earlier, before the servant has started sweeping, and he shouldn't really waste time sweeping, when he is being paid to do other work. If the boy is impervious to any sensible considerations, then at least the servant, that half-blind ancient, whom the boss would certainly not tolerate in any other section than Blumfeld's, and who hangs on there by the grace of God and the boss, then at least this servant could be a little gracious and leave his broom for a few moments with the boy. He's so clumsy anyway, he will lose heart right away and before you know it will be imploring the servant to take over. But just at the moment the servant seems to feel particularly responsible for the sweeping. You can see that, the instant the boy goes up to him, he clutches the broom more tightly in his trembling hands. He prefers to stand where he is and stop sweeping, just so as to concentrate all his attention on his ownership of the broom. The junior now no longer asks with words, because he does have some fear of Blumfeld, who appears to be doing sums; also ordinary words would be unavailing, because the servant can only be reached with very loud shouts. So the junior tugs at the servant's sleeves. The servant understands of course, and he gives the junior his fiercest glare, shakes his head, and pulls the broom closer to him, against his chest. Next the junior clasps his hands together and begs him. He doesn't have any hope of achieving anything by begging, but to do so amuses him, so he begs. The other junior accompanies the proceedings with subtle smiles and obviously thinks in some inexplicable way that Blumfeld is unable to hear him. The begging, indeed, fails to make the least impression on the servant, who turns round and thinks he is now able to use the broom with safety. But the junior has

followed him on tiptoe and, rubbing his hands together be-
seechingly, is now begging him from the other side. These
turns on the part of the servant and tiptoeings on that of the
junior are now repeated several times. Finally the servant
feels hemmed in on every side, and notices something that,
had he been a little less simpleminded, he might have realized right away, namely that he will tire before the junior
does. In consequence of which he seeks help from outside,
threatens the junior with his finger and points to Blumfeld
to whom, unless the junior desists, he will make a complaint. The junior sees now that if he wants the broom at
all, he will have to get a move on. So he makes a cheeky
grab for the broom. An involuntary cry from the other junior
signals the move. The servant this time manages to rescue
the broom by taking a step back, and taking the broom with
him. But now the junior knows no more forbearance: with
mouth agape and eyes flashing, he leaps after the servant,
who makes to flee, but his old legs instead of running merely
tremble. The junior rips at the broom, and even if he isn't
able to seize it, he does enough to make the broom clatter
to the ground, and thus become lost to the servant. Apparently to the junior as well, because as the broom falls all
three freeze—the two juniors and the servant—because now
Blumfeld must see what is going on. And in fact Blumfeld
does now look up out of his little window, as though only
just made aware of what was going on. Sternly and levelly he
looks them each in the eye, nor does the broom on the floor
escape him either. Whether it's that the silence has gone on
for too long, or that the guilty junior is unable to suppress
his desire to sweep, at any rate he stoops, very carefully admittedly, as though reaching for a wild animal and not a
broom, picks up the broom, passes it across the floor, then

straightaway throws it away in horror as Blumfeld jumps up and steps out of his little section.

"Get to work both of you, and stop mucking about," Blumfeld shouts, and with his extended hand he points the two juniors the way back to their desks. They obey, but not shamefaced and with lowered heads; instead, they stalk stiffly past Blumfeld, stare him in the eye, as though to keep him from hitting them. Experience might have taught them that Blumfeld never strikes, but they are overly timid and are forever crassly seeking to preserve their real or apparent rights.

The Bridge

I was rigid with cold; I was a bridge, lying suspended across a gully, here on this side were my toes, on the other my fingertips were drilled in, I had bitten myself fast in crumbling cement. The skirts of my coat were flapping around my sides. In the depths was the noise of the icy trout stream. No tourist ever wound up at this impassable height; the bridge was not yet marked in any map. So I lay and waited; I was bound to wait; short of falling, no bridge, once built, can ever cease to be a bridge. Once toward evening, it may have been the first or the thousandth, I don't know, my thoughts were always in a tangle, and forever going round and round, toward evening in summertime, the stream was rushing more darkly, I heard the footfall of a man. Now concentrate, concentrate. Stretch yourself, bridge, put yourself in order, unfenced struts, hold the one who has been entrusted to you, compensate discreetly for any uncertainties of his step, and then should he sway, make your presence felt, and like a mountain god, hurl him ashore. There he came, tapping me with the iron ferrule of his stick, then he flicked up the tails of my coat and brushed them straight over me, drove the point of his stick into my bushy hair and left it there, presumably while he looked away into the distance. Then—just as I was dreaming him over hill and dale—he suddenly jumped with both feet onto the middle of my body. I shuddered in wild pain, wholly at a loss. Who was this? A child? A gymnast? A daredevil? A suicide? A tempter? A destroyer! And I turned round to catch a sight of him. A bridge turns round. I hadn't completely turned when I was already falling, I was falling and already I was dashed to pieces and pierced on the pointed little rocks that had always gazed up at me so quietly from the rushing waters.

Texts on the Hunter Gracchus Theme

Two boys were sitting on the harbor wall playing dice. A man was reading the newspaper on the steps of a monument in the saber-swinging hero's shadow. A girl was filling her bucket at the well. A fruit vendor was lying beside his wares, staring out onto the lake. Through the empty door and window openings one could see two men over their wine in the depths of a bar. The landlord was sitting at a table nearer the front, drowsing. A barque swept quietly into the little harbor, as though being carried over the water. A man in a blue overall clambered ashore, and made the ropes fast to the rings. Two other men in dark jackets with silver buttons followed the bosun, carrying a bier on their shoulders, in which it was clear that, under a large tasseled silk cloth with flower patterns, a man was lying. No one on the quayside bothered about the new arrivals, even when they set down the bier to wait for the bosun, who was still working on the ropes; no one stepped up to them, asked them a question or gave them a closer look. The leader was a little further delayed by a woman who now appeared on deck, with loose hair and a child at her breast.

Finally the bosun was ready and indicated a yellowish two-story house whose straight lines could be seen on the left side of the waterfront; the bearers picked up their load and carried it through the low entrance formed by two slender pillars. A small boy opened a window, just caught the group disappearing into the house and hurriedly shut the window again. The door, made of heavy carved oak, was closed behind the party. A flock of pigeons that had been flying around the church tower now settled in front of the house. As though there was food waiting for them within, the pigeons collected in front of the gate. One flew up to the first floor and pecked at a windowpane. They were pale, well-looked-after, lively birds. With a magnificent gesture, the woman on the barque threw them some grain, which they picked up and flew over to the woman.

An old man in a top hat with mourning ribbon came down one of the little lanes that led steeply down to the harbor. He was looking attentively about him; everything seemed to perturb him—the sight of garbage in a corner made him frown, on the steps to the monument there were fruit peelings, which he pushed away with his stick in passing. He knocked on the pillared door, at the same time taking his top hat in his black-gloved hand. The door was opened right away. Some fifty small boys were lining the long corridor, and bowed. The bosun came down the stairs, greeted the gentleman and led him up the stairs. On the first floor the two men walked around the galleried patio, and while the boys followed behind at a respectful distance, the men entered a large cool room at the back that had no other building facing it, but a bare gray-black surface of rock. The bearers were busy setting up and lighting a few long candles at the head of the bier; but they shed no light, rather they shook up the shadows that had been in repose thus far, causing them to flicker over the wall. The cloth had been peeled back over the bier. Below it lay a man with a wild tangle of hair and beard, a tanned complexion and the appearance of a hunter. He lay there motionless, apparently not breathing, with eyes shut, and yet it was only the setting that seemed to suggest that he might be a corpse.

The gentleman strode up to the bier, laid his hand on the forehead of the man thus laid out, then knelt down and prayed. The bosun motioned to the bearers to leave the room and they went out, shooed away the boys who had collected outside and closed the door after them. For the gentleman, though, even this measure of silence seemed not to be enough. He looked at the bosun who understood and walked out through a side door into an adjacent room. Straightaway the man on the bier opened his eyes, turned to the gentleman with a painful half smile, and said: "Who are you?" Without visible surprise the gentleman got up off his knees, and replied: "The mayor of Riva." The man on the bier gave a nod, pointed with his feebly extended arm to a chair, and once the mayor had followed his invitation, said: "I knew of course, Mr. Mayor, but in the first instant I always forget, everything spins around in my head, and it's better that I ask, even if I know everything. You presumably know that I am the hunter Gracchus." "Indeed," said the mayor, "your coming was announced to me overnight. We were all asleep. Then toward midnight my wife called out: 'Salvatore'—that's my name—'look at the pigeon in the window.' It was a pigeon, but as big as a hen. It flew to my ear and said: 'Tomorrow the dead hunter Gracchus is coming, welcome him in the name of the town.'" The huntsman nodded, and moistened his lips with the tip of his tongue: "Yes, those pigeons fly ahead of me. Do you think I can stay in Riva, Mayor?" "I can't say yet," replied the mayor. "Are you dead?" "Yes," said the huntsman, "as you see. Many years ago, it must be an inordinate number of years ago now, I fell from a rock in the Black Forest, which is somewhere in Germany, while I was in pursuit of a chamois. Since then I've been dead." "But you're alive as well?" said the mayor. "In a certain sense," said the huntsman, "in a certain sense I'm alive as well. My skiff went astray, a wrong touch on the tiller, a moment's inattentiveness on the part of the bosun, distracted as he might have been by my beautiful homeland, I don't know what it was. All I know is that I remained on earth and that my skiff has since then been sailing earthly waters. I only ever wanted to live in the mountains; now after my death I am touring all the countries of the world." "And no part of you is in the Beyond?" asked the mayor with a frown. "I am," replied the huntsman, "always on the wide staircase that leads there. I am on that endlessly wide staircase, sometimes further up, sometimes further down, sometimes right, sometimes left, always in motion. If I take a great run-up, then I see the shining gates at the top, only to awaken in my old boat, stuck in some terrestrial waterway. My botched death grins at me in my cabin. Julia, the bosun's wife, knocks and brings me the morning beverage of whatever coast we happen to be passing." "A terrible fate," said the mayor with hand upraised as though to ward it off. "And you're not at fault at all?" "Not at all," said the hunter, "I was a hunter, is that perhaps my fault? I was engaged as a hunter in the Black Forest; at the time there were still wolves. I lay in wait, I shot, I hit, I skinned carcasses, is that my fault? My work was blessed. I was called the great hunter of the Black Forest. Is that my fault?" "I'm hardly qualified to say," said the mayor, "but it doesn't seem to me that you were at fault. But then who was?" "The bosun," said the huntsman.

"So now you're proposing to stay with us in Riva for a while?" asked the mayor.

"I'm not proposing anything," said the hunter, smiling, and laid his hand placatingly on the mayor's knee. "I'm here, that's all I know, that's all I can do. My skiff is without a rudder; it sails with the wind that blows in the lowest regions of Death."

I am the hunter Gracchus, my home is the Black Forest in Germany.

No one will read what I am writing here; no one will come to my help; if the instruction went out to help me, then all the doors of all the houses would remain locked, and all the windows; everyone would lie in their beds with the covers pulled over their heads, the whole world like an inn at night. There is every reason for this, because no one knows me, and if they knew me, then they wouldn't know where I was, and if they knew where I was, then they wouldn't know if I was going to stay there, and if they knew I was going to stay there, then they wouldn't know how to help me. The idea of helping me is a disease that needs to be cured in bed.

I know all this, and so I'm not writing to ask for help, even if there are moments when, undisciplined as I am, I think about it very hard, as, for instance, right now. But it's enough to rid me of any such ideas if I look around and see where I am and where—I think I'm right in saying—I've been living for hundreds of years. As I write this, I'm lying on a wooden pallet, I'm wearing—it's no comfort to look at myself—a dirty shroud, my hair and beard are a tangle of gray and black, my legs are wrapped in a large, long-tasselled silk shawl with flower patterns. By my head a church candle sheds a little light. On the wall facing me there's a small picture, evidently of a Bushman, who is aiming his spear at me and taking cover behind a magnificent painted shield. You run into some stupid pictures on board ship, but this is really one of the stupidest. The balmy air of the southern night comes through a porthole in the side, and I can hear the water splashing against the sides of the old barque.

I've been lying here since the time when, still the living huntsman Gracchus, I was pursuing a chamois in my native Black Forest and plunged to my death. Everything happened by the book. I gave chase, I fell, I bled to death in a gorge, I was dead, and this barque was supposed to carry me into the Beyond. I can still remember how cheerfully I first stretched out on this pallet; the hills had never heard such singing from me, as these four still-twilit walls. My life had been a happy one, and I had died happily; happily before going on board I cast aside my rifle, my bag and huntsman's tunic, that I had always worn proudly, and slipped into my shroud as proudly as a girl might slip into her wedding dress. Here I lay and waited.

Then

───────────────

"Is it true, Huntsman Gracchus, that you have been drifting for centuries in this old skiff?"

"For fifteen hundred years."

"And always on this boat?"

"Always on this boat. 'Barque' is the proper designation. Do you not know your shipping terms?"

"No, I've not had occasion to before today, when I first heard of you and set foot on your boat."

"Don't apologize. I'm a landlubber myself. No mariner, nor ever wanted to be; the woods and mountains were all my joy and now—the oldest sailor in the world, huntsman Gracchus, patron saint of mariners, huntsman Gracchus fervently prayed to by terrified cabin boys in stormy nights up in the crow's nest. Don't laugh."

"Laugh? I'm not laughing. I stood with pounding heart at the door to your cabin, with pounding heart I went in. Your friendly nature eases me a little, but never will I forget whose guest I am."

"That's right. Whatever happens, I'm the huntsman Gracchus. Don't you want some wine, I don't know what sort it is, but it's heavy and sweet, the boss looks after me well."

"Not now, if you don't mind, I'm too anxious. Maybe later, if you let me stay that long. Who is the boss?"

"The owner of the barque. These bosses are most excellent

people. I just don't understand them very well. I don't mean their language, although I often don't understand that either. That's just by the by. I've learned enough languages over the centuries that I could be an interpreter between the ancestors and people today. But I don't understand the thinking of these ships' owners. Perhaps you could explain it to me."

"I don't hold out much hope of that. How could I explain something to you, when relative to you I'm like a babe in arms?"

"Well, not like that. And you'll be doing me a favor if you come over with a little more confidence, a little more manliness. What will I do with a shadow for a guest? I'll blow him out of the porthole into the lake. I need explanations for all sorts of things. You, as someone on the outside, could furnish me with some. But if you sit here at my table quaking and through false modesty forgetting what little you knew anyway, then you might as well pack up. I'm a straight from the shoulder guy."

"There's something in what you say. There are probably things I can help you with. I'll try and get a grip on myself. Ask away."

"Better, much better, you exaggerate the opposite way and come up with some imaginary superiority. Understand me. I'm a person same as you, just a couple of centuries older and more impatient. So, let's talk about ships' owners. Pay attention. And have a drink to sharpen your senses. Don't hold back. Fill your boots. There's more in the hold."

"Gracchus, the wine is delicious. Here's to the patron."

"Too bad he died today. He was a good man, and he died in peace. Tall, well-grown children stood at his deathbed, and at the foot end his wife fell down in a dead faint. His last thought was of me. In Hamburg. He was a good man."

"Good Lord, in Hamburg, and you already know that he passed away today?"

"What? How would I not know when my patron dies? You're a little simpleminded."

"Are you out to offend me?"

"No, not at all, I'm most reluctant to do so. But you should be less startled, and drink more. And as far as patrons go, it's like this: to begin with the barque didn't belong to anyone."

"Gracchus, a favor, please. Will you tell me briefly and coherently about your situation? I have to admit, I don't understand it. As far as you're concerned, it's all self-evident, and in that way of yours, you assume the whole world knows about it. But in a short life—for life is short, Gracchus, try to remember that—in this short life, we have our work cut out to keep ourselves and our families. So, however interesting a figure huntsman Gracchus is—and that's the truth, not flattery—we don't have time to think about him, make inquiries about him, or worry about him. Maybe on our deathbed, like your Hamburg man, I don't know. Maybe that's when the hardworking man has a moment to stretch out for the first time and in among the leisurely processes of his thoughts there may be some of the green huntsman Gracchus. Other than that, though, as I say, I hadn't heard of you. I am here in port on business, I saw the barque, the gangplank was down, I climbed up it—but now I'd like to hear something detailed and coherent about you."

"Oh, coherence, that old canard. All the books are full of it, in all the classrooms the teachers are chalking it up on the blackboard; the mother dreams of it while her baby is at her breast—and there you are, sitting here, asking me about coherence. You must have had an unusually misspent youth."

"Possibly so, most youths are. But I think it would be very useful to you to take a look about you in the world. It may appear droll to you, I'm almost surprised at it myself, but it's right, isn't it, you're *not* the talk of the town. Whatever people talk about here, you're not among them; the world goes its merry way, and you're on your cruise, but before today I've never noticed your appearance anywhere."

"Those are your observations, my dear fellow, other people have made different ones. There are two possibilities. Either you're keeping quiet about what you know about me, and you intend something thereby. In that case I will simply say: you're making a mistake. Or again, you really don't remember me, because you're confusing my story with someone else's. In that case, I say to you: I am—no, I can't, everyone knows it, and yet I'm supposed to tell it to you! It all happened such a long time ago. Ask the chroniclers! They sit in their rooms with their mouths hanging open, looking at things in the dim and distant, and describing it without cease. Go and ask them, and then come back. It's all such a long time ago. How can I keep it in my overstuffed brain?"

"Wait, Gracchus, I can make it easier for you. I'll ask you questions. Where are you from?"

"From the Black Forest, as everybody knows."

"Of course, from the Black Forest. And that's where you were a huntsman in, let's see, the fourth century."

"Hey, have you been to the Black Forest?"

"No."

"Then you really don't know anything. The bosun's infant son knows more than you do, but really, much more. I wonder who brought you in here. It feels like fate to me. It seems your initial modesty was only too well grounded. You're a nothing that I'm filling full of wine. It turns out you don't even know the Black Forest. I was a huntsman there until my twenty-fifth year. If that chamois hadn't tempted me—there, now you know—then I would have had a long and happy huntsman's life, but the chamois tempted me, and I fell to my death on the rocks. And now here I am, dead, dead, dead. I don't know what I'm doing here. I was loaded up on the barque in the proper fashion, a poor stiff, I suffered the usual three or four things to be done to me as they are for everyone else, why make an exception of huntsman Gracchus, everything was in order, I lay stretched out on the skiff—

Yesterday There Came to Me
a Swoon . . .

Yesterday there came to me a swoon. She lives in the house next door, I have seen her disappear in there often enough in the evenings, hunching over in the low gateway. A large lady in a long flowing dress and wide-brimmed hat decorated with feathers. She came rushing up to my door like a doctor afraid of arriving too late to his fading patient's bedside. "Anton," she called out in her hollow and somehow theatrical voice, "I'm on my way, I'm here." She dropped into the chair I indicated to her. "You live so high up," she said plaintively, "so high up." The steps skipped before my eyes, innumerable steps leading up to my room, one after the other, little indefatigable waves. "Why so cold?" she asked, pulled off her old fencer's gauntlets, tossed them onto the table, and twinkled at me, her head a little to one side. I felt I was a sparrow, practicing my skips on the stairs, and she was tousling my soft, fluffy, gray feathers. "I'm so terribly sorry you're eating yourself up about me. I have often looked with real sadness into your pining face as you stood in the courtyard gazing up at my window. Now I am not unfavorably disposed to you, and while you may not have my heart yet, you will surely be able to conquer it."

I Really Should Have ...

I really should have paid a little more attention to these stairs before now, to the local conditions and ramifications, what to expect and how to react. But you never heard the least thing about these stairs, I said to myself by way of apology, and in newspapers and books they're forever discussing all sorts of topics. But never anything about these stairs. That's as may be, I replied to myself, you will have been reading absentmindedly. How often you were distracted, left out whole paragraphs, or just read the headlines; maybe the stairs were in there somewhere, and it escaped you; and now you need the very thing that escaped you. And I stood still for a moment and considered that as an objection. Then I thought I could remember reading about some similar stairs, perhaps in a children's book. It wasn't much, perhaps nothing more than a passing reference to their existence, and that was no good to me at all.

Building the Great Wall of China

The Great Wall of China has been completed at its northeast point. The construction advanced from the southeast and the southwest and was joined here. This same system of partial construction was also adopted in microcosm, within the two great armies of laborers in the East and the West. The pattern was this: gangs numbering a score or so of laborers were formed, and each was made responsible for a section of five hundred yards, while another gang was set to build a section of a similar length to meet theirs. After the two had met, the construction wasn't taken up at either end of the thousand yards; rather the gangs were reassigned to other sites in other places far away. The inevitable outcome was a plethora of large gaps which were only filled in by and by, some of them even after the successful completion of the entire project had been announced. Yes, there are said to be some gaps that have seen no construction at all; according to some sources, they are far larger than the built sections, a claim, though, that may merely be another one of the numerous legends that attend the project, and in view of its vast extent are unsusceptible of proof by a single human being and a single pair of eyes and his own measurements. One might have taken it as a given that it would have been advantageous in every way to build continuously, or at least continuously within the two principal sections. The purpose of the wall was, after all, as is generally claimed and known to be the case, protection against tribes to the north. How can a discontinuously built wall afford any protection? Not only can such a wall afford no protection, the construction itself is in continual danger. Abandoned sections of wall in remote places can easily and repeatedly be destroyed by nomads, not least as, having been initially intimidated by the construction, they changed their abode like locusts, with baffling rapidity, and perhaps had a better view of the progress of the work as a whole than we who were building it.

Even so, the building could probably not have been carried out in any other way. To understand this, one should bear the following in mind: the wall was to serve as a protection for hundreds of years, so very methodical construction, use of the expertise of all known ages and peoples, continuing sense of personal responsibility of the workers, all these were givens. Lesser tasks might be performed by ignorant day laborers drawn from the mass of the people—men, women, and children—whoever applied for good money could be made use of, but even someone in charge of four day laborers needed to be a qualified builder, a man capable of sensing what was at stake down to the roots of his being. And the greater the responsibility, the greater, evidently, the demands made of him. Such men were indeed available, albeit not in the numbers the project could have used. We had not approached the task in any way frivolously. Fifty years before the beginning of the construction, throughout the length and breadth of the China that was to be walled about, the art of building,

and bricklaying in particular, had been declared a strategi-
cally valuable science, and all other things only inasmuch as
they stood in some relation to it. I still remember very well
how, as small toddlers, we stood in our teacher's little garden
and were told to build a wall of pebbles; the way the teacher
wrapped the skirts of his coat about him, ran against our wall,
of course knocked everything flying, and denounced us so
bitterly for the feebleness of our work that we ran home crying to our parents. A tiny incident, but indicative of the mood
of the times. I was fortunate in that, when I passed my final
school exams at the age of twenty, the building of the wall
was just beginning. I say fortunate because many others who
had previously attained the apex of the education available to
them, their heads full of grandiose building plans, found they
had nothing to do and became useless drifters. But those who
were able to join the project as foremen, albeit on the lowest
grade, were genuinely worthy of the distinction. They were
men who had done a lot of thinking about building and didn't
stop thinking about it either, who from the first stone they
set in the earth felt, so to speak, at one with the construction.
Such men were of course driven by the desire to give of their
very best, as well as by an impatience to see the wall finally
completed. The day laborer was unacquainted with such impatience, he was driven only by his wages; while the higher-
ups, yes, even middle-ranking engineers saw enough of the
manifold growth of the project to keep their spirits resilient,
but the foremen, intellectually vastly overqualified for their
apparently modest tasks, required care of a different sort. It
wasn't possible to take them and replant them, for instance,
in some uninhabited mountain region hundreds of miles
from their home, and have them set stones by the month
or even by the year; the hopelessness of such assiduous, but

even over a long life inconclusive labor would have rendered them desperate and reduced the value of their work. Hence the system of partial construction was adopted: five hundred yards could be completed in roughly five years, by the end of which the foremen would usually be exhausted and have lost all confidence in themselves, the construction and the world in general; then, while they were still feeling the elation of the celebrations of the coming together of the thousand yards, they were sent somewhere far away, saw on their travels occasional completed parts of the Wall soar up, passed through the quarters of senior managers, who presented them with official medals, heard the cheers of the new armies of laborers streaming out from the interior, saw forests leveled for scaffolding, saw mountains quarried to stones, heard in the holy sites the songs of the faithful praying for the successful completion of the construction—and all this soothed their impatience; the quiet domesticity to which they had been temporarily restored strengthened them; the high regard in which everyone associated with the project stood, the fervor and humility with which their reminiscences were listened to, the trust that the quiet ordinary citizen put in the ultimate completion of the Wall, all this kept the strings of their souls taut. Like eternally optimistic children, they said goodbye to home, their desire to do the people's work became irresistible, they left home earlier than they had to, half the village accompanied them, on all the roads there were farewells, banners, and flags, never before had they seen how rich and beautiful and large and admirable their country was, every fellow citizen was a brother, for whom they were building the protective wall and who would thank them with everything they had and for as long as they lived, Unity, Unity, shoulder to shoulder, a popular dance, blood, no longer trapped in the sluggish circulation of a single body, but rolling sweetly and endlessly through our Middle Kingdom.

And that was the explanation for the system of partial construction, but there were other reasons for it besides. Nor is it odd that I should spend so much time debating this issue—however specialized it may at first appear, it's close to the heart of the whole project. If I am to give a sense of the thinking and the experience of those times, then it is not possible to investigate this particular matter too deeply.

It is surely correct to say that feats were accomplished at that time that bear comparison to the Tower of Babel, though in terms of pleasingness to God, at least as far as we humans can tell, they had the opposite tendency. I say as much, because early on during the construction a scholar published a book in which such a comparison was specifically made. He tried to argue that the Tower of Babel remained uncompleted not because of the generally claimed reasons, or at least those were not the major ones. His evidence came not from writings and reports; rather, he pursued his investigations on location. In the course of them he found that the structure suffered from weakness in its foundations and was therefore doomed to collapse. In this respect at least, our time was far superior to that distant era: almost every educated person was a professional mason and an expert in the science of foundations. This was not the scholar's objective, though; instead he claimed that the Great Wall would for the first time in history make a sure foundation for a new Tower of Babel. First the Wall, and then the Tower. The book was in everyone's hands at the time, but I must confess that even today I don't quite understand how he conceived of his Tower. Our Wall, which was not even circular, but at best a sort of quarter- or semicircle, was to make the foundations for a tower? That could only be meant in a sort of figurative way. But then what of the actual Wall, which was the outcome of the endeavors and the lives of hundreds of thousands? And why did the work come with blueprints, admittedly rather vague, in which the Tower was sketched, and suggestions—quite detailed, at times—as to how the strength of our people might be brought to bear on the new project? There was a lot of confusion at the time—that book is only one example—perhaps because the attempt was being made to focus the efforts of so many on one objective. Human nature, ultimately footloose as it is, of the quality of a puff of dust, will not stand for much in the way of commitment; if it finds itself committed, then it will shake at its fetters like mad, and will ultimately tear apart wall and chain and itself and scatter everything to the four winds.

It is possible that these arguments, ultimately against the building of the Wall, were then incorporated by the leadership in their strategy of partial construction. It was only when we—and I speak in the name of many others here— puzzled out the instructions of senior management that we got to know ourselves and found that without their leadership neither our training nor our psychological gifts would have been enough even for the tiny part we took up in the whole. In the counsels of management—no one I asked knew or knows where they met or who was there—but surely all human thoughts and drives were weighed in these counsels, and balanced against them all human aims and fulfillments; while through the window the reflection of divine worlds fell on our leaders' hands as they drew up their plans.

And so the honest observer refuses to believe that the leadership, if they had seriously purposed such a thing, could not also have surmounted those difficulties attendant on a holistically conceived Wall. There remains only the conclusion that the leadership had set its heart on the method of partial building. But partial building was a makeshift tactic and not really fit for purpose. So the leadership *wanted* something not fit for purpose. A curious conclusion, I daresay. And yet it has some things going for it too. It may be possible today to talk of it without danger. At that time it was a secret principle of many, among them many of the best: try with all your might to understand the orders of the leadership, but only up to a certain point, and then stop thinking. A sensible principle that also found expression in a parable that later gained currency: stop thinking, not because it could harm you; stop thinking because it is by no means certain that it could harm you. It is wrong in fact to speak of things as harming or not-harming. You will be as the river in spring. Its level rises, it gets bigger and stronger, it irrigates the land beyond its banks more effectively, it keeps more of its own being further out to sea, it will resemble the sea and be more welcome to it. To that extent, try to follow the orders of the leadership. But then the river bursts its banks, loses form and definition, slows its current, seeks against its nature to form little inland lakes and damages pastureland; and yet in the long run it fails to keep its present extent, but retreats to its original course; yes, in the ensuing dry spell it even starts to shrink miserably: do not try to think through the instructions of the leadership to that degree.

Now this comparison may have been extraordinarily relevant during the time of the construction of the Wall, but for my present report it is of limited use. The nature of my investigation is historical; the storm clouds have long since scattered and produce no more lightning, and I am free to seek an explanation for the partial construction that goes beyond the one with which we had to content ourselves at the time. The bounds of my thinking are narrow enough, while the terrain they flow through is limitless.

Now, against whom was the Great Wall supposed to afford protection? Against the peoples of the north. I come from the southeast of China. No northern peoples menace us here. We read about them in old books; the cruel acts their nature compels them to commit cause us to sigh in our peaceful pergolas; in paintings from life we see the devilish faces, the gaping mouths, the jaws studded with teeth sharpened to a point, the slits of eyes that seem to narrow at the prospect of loot which they will rend and grind in their mouths. If our children are restive, we show them such pictures and they fling themselves crying around our necks. But that is all we know of these Northerners. We have never seen them, nor will we ever see them if we remain in our villages, even if they drive and whip their wild horses straight toward us; the country is too big and won't give them access to us, they will be scattered in the empty air.

So, if all this is the case, why do we leave our homes, our rivers and bridges, our mothers and fathers, our weeping spouses, our children who need instruction, and move away to study in the faraway city, and our thoughts still further away, with the Wall to the north. Why? Ask our leaders. They know us. They, who grapple with huge anxieties, know us, know our small businesses, see us huddle together in our low huts, and the prayer the head of household says in the evening in the circle of the family either pleases or displeases them. And if I may be permitted such a thought about our leadership, then I must say, in my opinion the leadership was preexistent—they did not come together like a group of high mandarins, stimulated by a happy morning dream, hurriedly summoned to a session, hurriedly taking a decision, and later that evening the populace drummed out of bed to carry out the decisions, even if it was merely to put on a show of fireworks to the glory of a divinity who yesterday showed favor to the gentlemen, only the next day, no sooner are the paper lanterns extinguished, to have them beaten up in a dark corner somewhere. The leadership has always existed, and the decision to build the Wall likewise.

My field of study during the building of the Wall and subsequent to it, right up to the present day, has been comparative ethnography—there are certain questions one can only get at by this means—and I have discovered that while we Chinese have certain popular national institutions in a uniquely clear form, we have others in unique obscurity. I have always wondered why, about the latter especially, and the building of the Wall is closely involved with these questions.

Among our murky institutions, one of the murkiest is certainly the Empire itself. In Peking, of course, and certainly at court, there may be some clarity on the subject, though that too is more apparent than actual: university professors of constitutional law and history claim to know all about these things, and to be able to transmit their knowledge to their students; and the further down the educational scale one goes, the more, reasonably enough, doubts disappear as to one's own knowledge, and a kind of quasi education washes around a few centuries-old statements that may have lost nothing of their eternal verity, but remain permanently indistinct in the haze and fog that enshroud them.

But of all things, the Empire is in my view something the people need to understand, seeing as they are where ultimately it draws its support. Here I am, once again, only qualified to talk about my home district. Apart from the agricultural deities and their worship that so variously and beautifully fills the calendar, all our thinking has always been focused on the Emperor. But not the current incumbent, or, if you like, him as well, if we had known him, or even the least thing about him. We were always at pains— it was the only curiosity we knew—to discover something about him. But, odd as it may sound, it was scarcely possible to learn anything: not from the pilgrims who crisscross our country or in nearby or distant villages; not from the sailors who come down not just our little local rivulet but the great and holy arteries of the land. That is, we were told many things, but received little information. So great is our country, no fairy tale can match its greatness—the heavens can barely stretch to cover it. And Peking itself is just a dot, the imperial palace a smaller dot. Admittedly, the Emperor as a concept looms as large as all the stories of the world. The living Emperor, though, is a human being no different from ourselves: he lies as we do in a bed, perhaps more lavishly proportioned, but still comparatively narrow and short. Just like us, he likes to have a good stretch, and if he happens to be very tired, then he yawns with his delicately shaped mouth. But how would we hear about it thousands of miles to the south, almost as far as the Tibetan plateau? Besides, any news, even if it were to reach us, would come far too late, would be long since out of date. The Emperor is clustered about with the shining and yet somehow opaque mass of the court, which is the counterweight to the Empire, and always trying with its poisoned arrows to shoot the Emperor off his perch. The Empire is immortal, but an individual Emperor may fall and die; even whole dynasties finally collapse and breathe their last in the death rattle of a single individual. Of such battles and sufferings the people will never get to hear—like strangers in a city, like latecomers, they stand at the back of densely crowded side streets, calmly eating their packed lunches, while a long way in front of them on the market square the execution of their overlord is in progress.

There is a legend that admirably sums up the relationship. The Emperor has, so it is claimed, sent you a message on his deathbed, to you—you alone, you miserable subject, the tiny shadow fleeing as far as it can from the imperial sun. He has asked the messenger to kneel down at his bedside and whispered the message in his ear; and it mattered to him so much that he had the man say it back to him. By nodding, he affirmed that that was what he had said. And before all the massed spectators at his dying—all the obstructing walls have been knocked through and on the wide and lofty staircase the great figures of the Empire stand in a circle—with all these people watching, he has dispatched his envoy. The envoy set off without delay, a strong man, tireless, a champion swimmer; now putting out one arm, now the other, he clears a way through the crowd; if he encounters resistance, he points to the emblem of the sun displayed on his chest; he gets ahead easily, better than anyone else. But the crowds are so great; their abodes are never-ending. If a path opened before him, how he would fly, and ere long you would hear the majestic pounding of his fists on your door. But instead, how futile are his efforts; still he is forcing his way through the apartments of the inner palace; never will he have put them behind him; and if he succeeded there, still nothing would have been won; he would have to cross the courtyards; and after the courtyards, the second, outer palace; further staircases and courtyards; another palace; and so on for thousands of years; and once he finally plunged through the outermost gate—but this can never be—then the imperial city would still lie ahead of him, the center of the world, piled high with its detritus. No one can make his way through there, much less with a message from a dead man to one of no consequence. Meanwhile, you will sit at your window and dream of it as evening falls.

In just this way, with this mixture of hope and hopelessness, do our people view the Emperor. They don't know which Emperor is ruling, and there are even some doubts as to the name of the dynasty. At school, many such things are learned parrot-fashion, and the general uncertainty in this regard is so great that even the best pupil is drawn into it. In our villages, long since deceased emperors are returned to the throne, and one who lives on only in song recently issued a proclamation, which the priest read aloud at the altar. Battles from our prehistory are being fought now, and with shining cheeks the neighbor charges into your house with the news. The imperial womenfolk, overstuffed on overstuffed cushions, seduced away from the old moralities by canny flatterers, swelling in bossiness, excitable with greed, sprawling in lust, rehearse their misdeeds; the more time has passed, the more garishly all the colors shine, and with loud lamentations the village one day gets to hear how thousands of years ago, an Empress once drank her husband's blood in great draughts.

This is how our people deals with its past, but the present can also get mixed in with the dead. If once, once in a lifetime, an imperial official calls in on the village on his tour of the province, makes some demands on behalf of whoever is ruling, checks the tax rolls, visits the school, questions the priest about our moral conduct, and then puts everything, just before he gets into his litter, into one long exhortation to the assembled community, then a smile will pass over our faces, sly looks are exchanged and we bend down to the children, so as not to be spotted by the official. How is it possible, we think, he speaks of one of the dead as though he were alive, this particular Emperor has died long ago, the dynasty has become extinct, the official is pulling our leg, but we pretend not to notice, we don't want to give offence. But serious obedience is due only to our current master: anything else would be sinful. And behind the quickly vanishing litter of the official, someone climbs out of a long crumbled urn and starts to throw his weight about as master of the village.

If someone concluded from such episodes that basically we have no Emperor, then that would not be too far from the truth. I must repeat: there is perhaps no more loyal people than ours in the south, but our loyalty is of no benefit to the Emperor. The little pillar at the entrance to the village may have the holy dragon on it, blowing in reverence its fiery breath in exactly the direction of Peking ever since anyone can remember, but Peking is as remote to the people in the village as the afterlife. Does such a village really exist, where the houses are packed together, covering the fields, further than the view from our hill can stretch, and between these houses day and night nothing but people, one head by another? It is easier to imagine a city like that than it is to believe Peking and its Emperor were one single thing, perhaps a cloud, calmly wandering under the sun with the passing of the ages.

The consequence of such beliefs is a sort of chaotic, ungoverned life. Not at all immoral; rarely in the course of my travels have I met with such moral purity as here at home. But it is a life that is subject to none of the current laws and obeys only the instructions and warnings issued to us from the olden days.

I am wary of generalizations, and won't claim that the situation is the same in all ten thousand villages in our province, let alone in all five hundred provinces of China. But perhaps on the basis of the many documents I have read on this subject, and on the basis of my own observations—particularly during the building of the Wall, the human material gave the sensitive observer a chance to understand the souls of almost every province—on the basis of all this I may perhaps be allowed to say that the prevailing view of the Emperor inevitably shows similarities with the view taken by my home village. I don't want to claim that such a view is correct, on the contrary. For the most part it is conditioned by the government, which, in the oldest empire in the world has thus far proved unable—or from pressure of other business has neglected—to establish the institution of the Empire in a sufficiently clear form that it might directly and uninterruptedly hold sway as far as its furthest frontiers. On the other hand, it does show a weakness of the popular imagination or perhaps a lack of faith, if it does not succeed in raising the Empire from its sunkenness in Peking in all its life and presence and pressing it to the breasts of its subjects, who desire nothing more than once to feel this embrace and die in its bliss.

Such a state of affairs cannot be for the good. All the more striking, then, that this weakness, this flaw, seems to be one of the most important sources of unity in our people; yes, if you will allow me to risk the expression, positively the ground on which we have our being. To set out a blemish in such detail here is not to shake our consciences, but, more importantly, our national structures. Therefore allow me for the moment not to pursue my exploration of this question any more at this stage.

This then was the world into which news of the Wall broke. It too was delayed by some thirty years after its original announcement. It happened one summer evening. I was ten years old, standing with my father on the river bank. In accordance with the significance of this often discussed moment, I remember the circumstances in the most minute detail. He was holding me by the hand, as he liked to do into his advanced old age, while running the other along the length of his very long thin pipe as though it were a flute. His long thin beard stuck out into the air, because in the enjoyment of his pipe he tended to gaze off into the distance across the river. And his pigtail, object of reverence among the children, rustling softly against the gold-embroidered silk of his festive garment, dangled accordingly low. Just then a barque stopped in front of us; the boatman waved to my father to come down the bank, as he himself set off up toward him. They met in the middle, the boatman whispered something into my father's ear; to get very close to him, he had even thrown his arm around him. I didn't manage to hear what was said—I only saw my father appear not to believe it, the boatman insist, my father still unable to believe it, the boatman with the passion of seafaring men everywhere trying to prove its truth by practically ripping the tunic across his chest, my father growing stiller and then the boatman clattering noisily back down to his barque and sailing away. Pensively my father turned toward me, knocked out his pipe, and stuck it in his belt, pinched my cheek and pulled my head closer to him. That was what I liked best of all, it made me very happy, and so we walked home together. The rice was already steaming on the table and the wine was just being poured into cups. Without seeming to notice these preparations, my father began to report from the threshold what he had been told. I do not remember any of the actual words, but the strangeness of the details communicated itself to me so strongly, even as a child, that I will try and reproduce them here. I will do so because it was very indicative of the popular comprehension. What my father said was this:

It Was One Summer . . .

It was one summer, a warm day. On the way home with my sister, we happened to pass the gate of a manor house. I don't know whether it was from pure mischievousness, or in a fit of absentmindedness that she struck the gate, or perhaps merely shook her fist at it and didn't strike it at all. A hundred paces further on, down the left-bearing road, a village began. It wasn't one we knew, but people came out of the first house, waving to us in a friendly way, but warning us at the same time, alarmed themselves, cringing with fear. They pointed to the manor we had passed, and referred us to the blow against the gate. The owners of the manor would bring charges against us, inquiries would begin straight away. I felt perfectly relaxed, and tried to calm my sister. She probably hadn't struck the gate at all, and even if she had, there was nowhere in the world where that would mean a trial. I tried to make the people around us see it that way, and they heard me but didn't give an opinion. Later on, they said that not only my sister but I too as her brother stood to be accused. I nodded and smiled. We were all of us looking back in the direction of the manor, the way you might look at a distant puff of smoke and wait for a flame to appear. And lo, before long we saw horsemen ride into the wide open gate, dust rise up, covering everything, and only the sharp points of lances flashing. No sooner had the troop disappeared into the courtyard than they seemed to have turned the horses and were on their way to us. I pushed my sister away, I would see that everything was cleared up; she refused to leave me. I told her she should at least change so as to appear in front of the gentlemen in a better dress. Finally she listened, and set off on the long way home. Already the riders were upon us, down from their horses they asked for my sister. She wasn't there just then, came the timid reply, but she would be along later. The answer was received almost with indifference; what seemed to matter was that I had been found. It was principally two gentlemen, the judge, lively young fellow, and his silent assistant whom he addressed as Assmann. I was asked to step into the front parlor of the inn. Slowly, moving my head from side to side, playing with my braces, I set off under the sharp eyes of the gentlemen. I almost thought a word might be enough to release me, a city boy, free and almost honorable, from these farm people. But as soon as I crossed the threshold, the judge who had gone on ahead, and was waiting for me, said: "I feel sorry for this man!" It was beyond doubt that he meant not my current state, but whatever lay in store for me. The parlor resembled a prison cell more than any rustic parlor. Large flagstones, dark gray bare walls, somewhere set in them an iron ring, in the middle something that looked half pallet, half operating table.

My Business ...

My business rests entirely on my shoulders. Two secretaries with typewriters and ledgers in the anteroom, then my office with desk, cashbox, coffee table, armchair, and telephone—that's the whole setup. Simple to run the eye over, easy to run. I am young, and the business trundles along ahead of me, I don't complain. I don't complain. Just after New Year, a young man moved into the empty premises next to mine that I had foolishly refused for a very long time to rent myself. Another room and anteroom, and a little kitchenette as well. I could surely have used the two offices—my two secretaries occasionally feel a little cramped—but then what would I have done with the kitchenette? That was the silly anxiety that kept me from taking it. Now I've got the young man sitting there. Harras, his name is. I don't know what he does. All it says on the door is "Harras, Office." I've made inquiries, and people told me he has a business along much the same lines as mine, there was no reason to advise against giving him a loan, he's an ambitious young man, whose business may be on an upward path; on the other hand, they wouldn't go so far as to recommend investing in him, because by all appearances he had no capital.

The usual advice you give when you don't know anything. Sometimes I run into Harras on the stairs: he always seems to be in a tearing rush, he shoots past me, so I've not really ever had a proper look at him. He has his office key ready in his hand, and in a trice he's opened the door and slipped in like the tail of a rat, and I'm standing in front of that name-plate again, "Harras, Office," which I've clapped eyes on much more often than I'd like to have done. The wretched plywood walls that betray the honest man of business and shield the dishonest one. My telephone is mounted on the party wall, but I mention that mostly in a spirit of irony, because even if it was on the other side of the room, you would still be able to hear everything that goes on. I've given up using the names of my clients on the telephone, but of course it doesn't take much to establish them from certain characteristic but unavoidable turns of phrase. Sometimes, with the earpiece at my ear, a martyr to my restlessness, I dance around the machine on tiptoe, but still can't keep from betraying my secrets. Of course that causes my business decisions to be more uncertain, and my voice shaky. What is Harras up to while I'm telephoning? I might stretch a point, as I'm bound to do, and say: Harras doesn't need a telephone, he uses mine, he has slid his sofa against the wall and is listening, meanwhile I have to run to the telephone when it rings, take onerous decisions, perform great feats of persuasion, but above all, throughout the whole process, I am involuntarily reporting to Harras through the wall. Perhaps he doesn't even need to wait for the conversation to end, but gets up when he's heard enough, scurries through the city in his typical fashion, and before I've hung up the earpiece, he's already busy thwarting my plan.

A Cross-Breed

I have an unusual animal, half pussycat, half lamb. It's an heirloom that belonged to my father, though it has grown up mostly in my own lifetime: once it used to be much more lamb than cat, now it's an equal blend of both. It has a cat's head and claws, and the size and form of a lamb; the flickering, gentle eyes partake of both; the fur, which is soft and close-lying, the movements that combine skipping and creeping; it likes to curl up on the windowsill in the sun, and purr; it gambols about the meadow like mad, and can barely be caught; it runs away from cats and tries to attack lambs; on moonlit nights the eaves are its preferred route; it can't meow and is frightened of rats; it is capable of lurking by the chicken coop for hours on end, though it has never yet killed anything; I feed it fresh milk, that's what best agrees with it, it laps it up in long draughts through its tigerish teeth. Of course the children love it. Sunday mornings they are allowed to visit. I have the animal on my lap and they stand around and watch. They ask the most extraordinary questions, which no one can answer. Nor do I make any attempt to; I am content simply to show the animal off. Sometimes the children bring cats of their own, once they even turned up with a pair of lambs; but contrary to their expectations, there were no great scenes of recognition, the animals looked at each other calmly through their animal eyes, and evidently took the other's existence as a divinely ordained fact.

On my lap the animal knows neither fear nor persecution. It feels happiest when pressed against me; it is loyal to the family that has nurtured it. This is probably not unusual, just the natural instinct of an animal that has plenty of in-laws all over the planet, but maybe not one close blood relation, and to whom the protection it has found among us is something sacred. Sometimes I laugh when it sniffs at me, or twists between my legs and is inseparable from me. Not content with being lamb and cat, it almost wants to be a dog as well! I am quite serious about this. It has in itself both forms of nervousness, that of the cat and the lamb, quite different though they are. That's why it is almost bursting out of its skin. Perhaps the butcher's knife would come as a relief for the animal, but heirloom that it is, I am unable to oblige it.

K. Was a Great Juggler ...

K. was a great juggler. His act was perhaps a little monotonous, but there was no doubting its virtuosity, and so it remained a great draw. I well remember the first time I saw him perform, even though it was fully twenty years ago, and I was a small boy at the time. He arrived in our little town without any prior announcement and put on the show on the evening of his arrival. In the great dining hall of our hotel, a little space had been cleared around one table in the middle—that was all it took by way of preparation. In my memory, the hall was packed, but every child will think a room is packed if there are a few lights, a hubbub of grown-ups' voices, a waiter running back and forth and so on. I don't know why so many people should have turned out for this obviously rushed event, but in my memory the packed hall forms a major part of my impression of the performance.

New Lamps

Y esterday I visited company HQ for the first time. Our night shift had elected me as their spokesman and since the design and filling of our oil lamps both leave something to be desired, I was to go there to demand that these grievances be addressed. I was shown to the relevant office, knocked, and entered. A delicate young man, very pale, smiled at me from behind a big desk. He nodded liberally, excessively. I wasn't sure whether to sit down or not—there was a chair there, but I thought that on the occasion of my first visit I perhaps shouldn't sit, and so I made my case standing up. It turns out this modesty of mine created difficulties for the young gentleman, because he had to crane his neck and turn his face up to me if he wasn't to move his chair back, which he didn't want to do. Then again, try as he might, he was unable to incline his head sufficiently and so, all the time I was talking, he was squinting up at the ceiling, where I couldn't help but follow. When I was finished, he slowly got to his feet, patted me on the back, said: I see, I see, and pushed me into the adjacent office where a gentleman with a wild growth of beard had evidently been waiting for us, because there was no sign on his desk of any work, while an open glass door led out to a little garden clustered with flowers and shrubs. A brief whispered aside of not many words from the young man was enough to apprise the gentleman of our grievances. He stood up right away and said: Well now, my dear—I think he wanted to say my name, and I was already opening my mouth to introduce myself all over again, but he cut me off: There, that's all right, I know you very well— well, your petition or complaint is certainly justified, I and the gentlemen on the board would be the last people not to see that. The welfare of the workforce means more to us— believe me—than the health of the factory. And why not, indeed? The factory can be rebuilt any time, it's just money, who cares about money, whereas if a human being loses his life, then a human being loses his life, and there is a widow and orphans. Dear Lord, yes. So every proposal to bring in new safety measures, new relief, new comfort, new luxuries, is most welcome to us. Whoever comes to us with such is our man. So just you leave your suggestions here, we will pore over them in detail; should some other dazzling innovation be attached to them, I'm sure we won't omit it, and at the end of the process you'll get your new lamps. Now go and tell your people downstairs: we won't rest until we've converted your mineshaft into a drawing room, and either you will die in patent-leather slippers, or else you won't die at all. Now, good day!

An Everyday Confusion

An everyday incident, and the bearing of it an instance of everyday heroism: A. is concluding an important piece of business with B. in the neighboring village of H. He goes to H. for the preliminary discussion, gets there and back in ten minutes each way, and at home glories in his particular swiftness. The following day his presence is required in H. again, this time for the final sealing of the deal; since this is likely to take several hours, A. sets off early in the morning; even though all external conditions, at least inasmuch as A. is aware of them, are unchanged, this time it takes him ten hours to get to H. When he gets there in the evening, totally exhausted, he is told that B., in annoyance at A.'s failure to show up, had set off to A.'s village half an hour ago; they should have met each other on the road. A. is advised to wait; B. will surely be back very soon. But A., in a panic now about the deal, sets off for home right away. This time, without especially thinking about it, he covers the distance in a flash. At home he learns that B. had arrived early in the morning, before A.'s departure—yes, he had even seen A. in the gateway and reminded him of their business—but A. had said he was in a hurry and had no time. In spite of this baffling behavior on the part of A., B. had settled down to wait for A. He had asked repeatedly whether A. was back yet, but was still up in A.'s room. Happy to learn that he could still see B. and explain everything to him, A. runs up the stairs. He is almost at the top when he stumbles, ruptures a tendon and, almost beside himself with pain, incapable even of screaming, only whimpering in the dark, he hears and looks on as B.—it is unclear whether it is at a great distance or right next to him—stomps down the stairs in a towering rage and is never seen again.

The Truth about Sancho Panza

By the constant purveying of tales of chivalry and robbery, mostly in the hours of darkness, Sancho Panza, who incidentally never claimed any credit for it, was able over the course of several years so to deflect from himself the attention of his devil, whom he later dubbed Don Quixote, that that gentleman later went on to perform the most outrageous deeds, by which, however, in the absence of their designated object, who was to have been precisely Sancho Panza, no one came to grief. Gaily, though perhaps with a certain residual sense of responsibility, Sancho Panza agreed to follow this Don Quixote on his exploits and thereby had much great and instructive entertainment of him until his end.

The Silence of the Sirens

Proof that inadequate, even childish, means may help toward salvation.

To keep himself safe from the Sirens, Odysseus had stuffed his ears with wax and had himself bolted to the mast. Other travelers might have done the same thing from time immemorial (except for those who were tempted by the Sirens from a distance), but it was known throughout the world that this could not help. The song of the Sirens was sufficient to pierce even wax, and the passion of those they had seduced was enough to shatter more than chains and mast. Odysseus, though, was not thinking of this, although he might have heard about it, and he placed his confidence in his handful of wax and tangle of chains, and, in innocent joy at his little precautions, he set his course toward the Sirens.

Now the Sirens have a weapon that is still more terrible than their singing, which is to say their silence. It is not written, but surely it could have happened, that a man might escape from their singing, but not from their silence. The feeling of having prevailed over them with one's own strength, and the resulting sense of invincibility, cannot be successfully opposed by anything earthly.

And indeed, as Odysseus approached, these great singers were just then not singing, whether because they believed they could defeat this opponent only by their silence, or the sight of the blissful expression on the face of Odysseus, who had nothing on his mind but wax and chains, made them quite simply forget to sing.

Odysseus, though, didn't hear their silence, so to speak, he thought they were singing and he was prevented from hearing it; fleetingly, he saw the curves of their throats, their deep breathing, their teary eyes, their half-opened mouths, but thought it was all part of the unheard arias that were all around him. Before long, everything slid off him as his eyes gazed into the distance, the Sirens vanished, and just as he was physically closest to them, he was wholly unaware of them.

They, for their part, never more beautiful, shuddered and stretched, let their writhing hair blow in the wind, played with their claws on the rocks; they no longer wanted to seduce, only to watch the luster of Odysseus's great eyes for as long as they could.

If the Sirens had had any understanding, they would have been destroyed there and then, but as it was they remained, only Odysseus escaped them.

There is an appendix to the story. So wily, they say, was Odysseus, such a cunning fox, that even the goddess of fate couldn't penetrate his interior, perhaps—though that is impossible to understand with human comprehension—perhaps he really noticed that the Sirens were silent and merely offered them the performance here related as a sort of sop— to them and the gods.

A Society of Scoundrels

There was once a society of scoundrels, or rather not scoundrels per se, just ordinary, average people. They always stuck together. When one of them had perpetrated some rascally act, or rather, nothing really rascally, just averagely bad, he would confess it to the others, and they investigated it, condemned it, imposed penalties, forgave him, etc. This wasn't corrupt—the interests of the individual and the society were kept in balance and the confessor received the punishment he asked for. So they always stuck together, and even after their death they didn't abandon their society, but ascended to heaven in a troop. It was a sight of childlike innocence to see them flying. But since everything at heaven's gate is broken up into its component parts, they plunged down like so many rocks.

Visiting the Dead

I was visiting the dead. There was a large salubrious tomb—a few coffins were already standing there, but there was a lot of room left; two coffins stood open, they looked like unmade beds that had been recently vacated. A desk stood off to one side, so that I didn't notice it right away; a powerfully built man was sitting at it. In his right hand he held a pen. It seemed as though he had been writing and had just stopped; his left hand was toying with a shining watch chain in his waistcoat, and his head was inclined in its direction. A charwoman was sweeping, but there was really nothing to sweep.

In a fit of curiosity, I tweaked at the kerchief that shadowed her face. Only then was I able to see her. She was a Jewish girl I had known once. She had a broad white face and narrow dark eyes. As she smiled at me in her rags that were making an old woman of her, I said: "You must be putting on a performance?" "Yes," she said, "a little bit. You can tell, can't you?" But then she pointed to the man at the desk and said, "Now go and introduce yourself to him, he's the boss here. Until you've made yourself known to him, I can't really talk to you." "Who is he?" I asked, more quietly.

"A French nobleman," she said. "His name's de Poiton."
"What's he doing here?" I asked. "I don't know," she said,
"it's all a big mess. We're waiting for someone to put it all
in order. Is it you?" "Oh no," I said. "That's very sensible
of you," she said, "but now go and say hello to the boss."

So I went and bowed to him; since he didn't raise his
head—I just saw the tangle of white hair—I said "Good evening," but he still didn't stir; a small cat ran around the edge
of the table, it seemed to have jumped up from her master's
lap and disappeared back there. Perhaps he wasn't looking
down at his watch chain at all, but under the table. I wanted
to explain why I had come to him, but my acquaintance
tugged at my coattail and whispered, "That's enough."

With that, I was very satisfied. I turned to her and we
strolled through the tomb arm in arm. Only, her broom was
bothering me. "Put the broom away," I said. "No, please,"
she said, "let me keep it; you can see that tidying up here is
no sort of work, can't you? It really isn't, but I take certain
advantages from it that I don't want to be without. By the
way, will you be staying here?" she asked, changing the subject. "I'd be happy to stay for your sake," I said slowly. We
were now pressed tight like lovers. "Stay, oh, do stay," she
said. "I've been longing for you. It's not as bad down here
as you maybe think. And what do we care, we've got each
other." We went along in silence for a while; we no longer
had linked arms, we were holding each other in an embrace.
We walked along the main aisle, there were coffins to right
and left; the tomb was very large, certainly very long. It was
dark, but not completely, there was a kind of twilight which
tended to brighten a little in spots where we were and form
a little ring around us.

Suddenly she said, "Come on, I'll show you my coffin." That surprised me. "You're not dead," I said. "No," she said, "but to admit the truth: I don't know my way around here very well, that's why I'm so glad you've come. In a little while you'll understand everything; even now you probably see everything more clearly than I do. At any rate: yes, I have a coffin." We turned right down a side path, again between two rows of coffins. The layout of the place reminded me of a large wine cellar I'd once seen. On the way we passed a small, quickly flowing stream barely three feet wide. Then we reached the girl's coffin. It was fitted with a pretty lace-covered pillow. The girl sat down in it, and beckoned me to her, less with her index finger than with the expression in her eyes. "Sweet thing," I said, pulling off her kerchief and pushing my hand into her thick soft hair. "I can't stay with you yet. There's someone down here in the tomb I have to speak to. Won't you help me find him?" "Do you have to speak to him? Promises are all invalidated here," she said. "But I'm not from here." "Do you think you'll manage to get away?" "I'm sure," I said. "Then you shouldn't waste any time," she said. She looked under her pillow and pulled out a shirt. "This is my shroud," she said and passed it up to me. "I'm not wearing it, though."

Night

Buried in the night. The way you sometimes bury your head in reflection, so utterly buried in the night. All around, people are asleep. A little bit of playacting on their part, an innocent bit of deception to be doing it in houses, on firm beds under firm roofs, or sprawled on mattresses and sheets, under blankets; in reality they have gathered as they did then and later too on wild terrain, in a camp in the open, a vast number of people, an army, a tribe, under a cold heaven on a cold earth, thrown to the ground on which a moment before they stood, face to the ground, brow in the crooks of their arms, breathing regularly. And you, you're keeping watch, you're one of the sentries, you communicate with the next man by waving a burning stick from the driftwood fire beside you. Why do you keep watch? Someone has to keep watch, they say. Someone must be there—

Our Little Town

Our little town is situated nowhere near the border; the border is so far away that perhaps no one from here has ever been there, there are wild upland plateaux to cross, but also broad fertile valleys. To think of even a part of the way there is exhausting, and it's not possible to think of more than a part. There are great cities along the way as well, many times bigger than our little town. Ten little towns placed side by side, and another ten little towns crammed on top of them from above, won't make one of these enormous and densely packed cities. If you don't lose your way going there, then you are bound to lose your way in the cities, and to skirt them is impossible because of their size.

Even further than the border, if it's even possible to compare such distances—it's a little like saying a three-hundred-year-old man is older than a two-hundred-year-old man—much further than to the border is the route from our little town to the capital city. While we do from time to time get news of border wars, we hear almost nothing from the capital, we, the citizenry, I should say, because government officials have quite a good line to the capital; in two or three months they are able to get news from there, at least so they claim.

The odd thing, which repeatedly perplexes me, is how we in our little town are content to abide by instructions that are issued in the capital. For hundreds of years no political change has occurred that was instigated by us. In the capital city, meanwhile, supreme rulers have replaced one another, whole dynasties have been exterminated or deposed and new ones begun; in the previous century the capital city itself was destroyed, and another one founded far away from it, only to be destroyed itself and the old one rebuilt—but all this has had next to no impact on us. Our officials were always in post, the most senior ones came to us from the capital, the next grades down brought in from elsewhere, the lowest from our own midst, and so it remained, and it was good enough for us. The highest-ranked official is the senior tax inspector: he has the rank of colonel and is addressed as such. Today he is an old man, but I have known him for many years, because he was a colonel already when I was a child. To begin with, his career advanced apace, then it seems to have stalled, but for our little town his rank is quite sufficient, we wouldn't be able to cope with anything more exalted. When I picture him to myself, I see him sitting on the veranda of his house on the square, leaning back, with his pipe in his mouth. Above him the imperial flag is fluttering on the roof; while on the sides of the veranda, which is of a size that smaller military exercises may be held on it, the washing has been hung out to dry. His grandchildren, in attractive silk clothing, are playing around him; they are not usually allowed to play on the square, as the other children are considered unworthy, but they are drawn to it nonetheless, and like to push their heads between the bars of the railings and, when the other children are having an argument, they join in from above.

This colonel, then, is the ruler of our little town. I don't think he has ever shown anyone his credentials. He probably doesn't have any. Perhaps he really is a senior tax inspector, but is that all? His office is very important in the town, but for the citizens there are others that might be more important. We almost have the impression here that people are saying: "All right, you've taken away everything we have, why don't you take us away too?" But he hasn't seized power, and he isn't a tyrant either. It has been the way of things from the olden days that the tax inspector is the senior official, and the colonel follows that tradition as much as we do.

But even though he lives among us without too much in the way of distinctions, he remains set apart. If a deputation goes to him with a request, he stands there like a wall. There is nothing behind him—at the most one might think one heard a couple of distant whispering voices, but that's probably an illusion; at least for us, he signifies the limits of power. One can only see him in his official capacity. As a small boy, I was there once when a deputation of citizenry asked him for some government assistance, because the poorest slum district had recently burned to the ground. My father, the blacksmith, a respected figure in the community, was a member of the deputation and had taken me with him. This is in no way unusual—every Tom, Dick, and Harry tries to gain attendance—it's almost impossible to pick out the actual deputation from the crowds there; since such receptions usually took place on the veranda, there are also individuals who swarmed up ladders and scrambled over the balustrade to participate in events. The arrangement was such that about a quarter of the veranda was set aside for him, and the rest was filled by the crowd. A few soldiers stood guard, some of them flanking him in a semicircle. Basically, one man would have been enough, such is our fear of these soldiers. I don't know exactly where they are drawn from—it's certainly far from here—but they all resemble each other, they don't even really require a uniform to be identified.

They are short but vigorous men; the most striking thing about them is their strong teeth that seem to burst from their mouths, and then a certain twitch in their small slitty eyes. These two qualities have made them a terror to the children, though a delight as well, because they like nothing better than to be continually terrorized by those teeth and those eyes, and then to run away from them in dread. This dread is probably not completely gone from the adults, or at least it has left a sort of after-echo. Other things have contributed to it as well. The soldiers speak a dialect that is quite incomprehensible to us—they can hardly get used to the way we speak either—which produces a certain unapproachableness in them that corresponds to their character; they are so silent, serious, and rigid, they don't do bad things and yet the sense of badness emanating from them is almost unbearable. For instance, a soldier may walk into a shop, buy some small item and stand there leaning on the till, listening to the conversation, probably not understanding it, but looking as though he understood it. He himself doesn't say a word, just looks rigidly at the person speaking, then at the one listening, with his hand on the handle of the long knife in his belt. It's repugnant—you don't feel like talking, the shop empties, and only when it's completely empty does the soldier leave the premises. So, wherever the soldiers set foot, our lively populace falls silent. That's the way it was then as well. As at all official occasions, the colonel stood bolt upright and in his extended hands he held two bamboo poles. This is an ancient practice and means more or less: he supports the law, and the law supports him. Now everyone knows what to expect up on the veranda and yet each time we get a new fright, and this particular time furthermore the designated speaker did not want to begin: he was standing facing the colonel, but his courage left him and, making various excuses, he pushed back into the crowd. No other suitable party came forward to speak either—there was no shortage of unsuitable parties—there was a great confusion, and envoys were dispatched to various noted speakers among the citizenry. All this time the colonel stood there perfectly impassive, only his chest rose and fell noticeably as he breathed in and out. Not that he was breathing hard, he was just breathing very distinctly, in the same way as, for example, frogs breathe; only that they always do, whereas here it was unusual. I crept through the ranks of the grown-ups, and observed him through a gap between two soldiers until one of them shoved me away with his knee. By now the original speaker had collected himself and, stoutly propped up by two fellow citizens, he gave his speech. What was so moving was that throughout this serious speech, describing our tragedy, he kept smiling, a very humble smile, that tried vainly to elicit a smile in response on the face of the colonel. Finally he came out with his request—I think it was for tax relief for one year, but it may equally have been for cut-price timber from the imperial forests. Then he bowed low and held the bow, and so did everyone else bar the colonel, the soldiers and a few officials who were hovering around. What was ridiculous in the eyes of the child was the way the people on the ladders on the edge of the veranda climbed down a few rungs so as not to be spotted during this decisive pause, and contented themselves with peeking out from time to time just over the floor level of the veranda. This went on for a while, then an official, a little man, stepped up to the colonel, sought to rise up to his level on tiptoe, had something whispered in his ear—the colonel was still impassive, apart from the deep breathing—clapped his hands, whereupon all stood straight, and announced: "The petition has been rejected. Depart." An undeniable feeling of relief spread through the crowd who all made their way down. No one paid any particular regard to the colonel, who had become a human being again, like the rest of us; I just happened to see how in exhaustion he dropped his poles, which fell to the ground, collapsed into an armchair pushed into place by a couple of officials, and hurriedly jammed the pipe into his mouth.

This whole incident is by no means isolated—this is typically how things happen. Yes, there are instances now and again of petitions being approved, but in those cases it is as though the colonel had done so on his own initiative as a powerful individual, and it has—not literally, but in terms of the feeling of the thing—positively to be kept from the government. Now, in our little town, the eyes of the colonel, so far as we can tell, are the eyes of the government as well, but some sort of distinction is being made here that we can't quite understand.

In matters of importance, however, the citizenry may be assured of a rejection on every occasion. And the thing here is just as extraordinary, because we seem not to be able to do without this rejection, even though for us our application and its rejection is by no means a formality. In a continual spirit of freshness and earnestness, we make our way there and leave again, while not exactly strengthened and contented, then at least not shattered and exhausted.

There is, though, I have sometimes thought to observe, a certain age group that is not happy, and these are young people of between seventeen and twenty: young whippersnappers who from their perspective are unable to gauge the effect of a wholly insignificant or incipiently revolutionary thought. And it is among these that dissatisfaction has sneaked in.

On the Matter of Our Laws

Our laws are unfortunately not widely known: they are the secret of the small group of nobles who govern us. We are convinced that these old laws are scrupulously observed, but it remains vexing to be governed by laws one does not know about. I am not thinking here of various questions of interpretation and the disadvantages entailed when only certain individuals are able to participate in the interpretation and not the population as a whole. These disadvantages may not be all that great. The laws are so old, after all—centuries have worked on their interpretation, and even though this interpretation has in a sense itself become codified, surely there is a certain freedom of interpretation still possible, though it will be very limited. Moreover, the nobility has no reason to be influenced by self-interest against us because the laws were from the very beginning set down in favor of the nobility, the nobility is outside the law and that is why the laws seem to have been given exclusively into their hands. There is wisdom in this disposition—who could question the wisdom of the old laws?—but also a torment for the rest of us, presumably that is not to be avoided.

Even these seeming laws can only be guessed at. It is a tradition that they exist and were entrusted to the nobility as a secret, but it is no more than an old—and by virtue of its age, a plausible—tradition, nor can it be more, because the character of the law demands that their existence be a matter of secrecy. If we members of the people have from time immemorial attentively observed the actions of our nobles, possess treatises written about them by our forefathers, and have in a sense perpetuated them, and think we can discern principles that would appear to suggest this or that legal stipulation, and if we try to arrange ourselves a little in accordance with these most carefully sifted and ordered conclusions—then all this is most uncertain, nothing more than a game of reason, because perhaps the laws we try to guess at don't exist at all. There is a small political party that believes this and that seeks to prove that if a law exists, then its form can only possibly be: what the nobles do is the law. This party sees only arbitrary acts on the part of the nobility, and disdains the popular tradition that in its opinion has brought only slight, accidental advantages, along with a great deal of serious harm, since they have given the people a false sense of security in relation to coming events. This harm is undeniable, but the large majority of our people see its cause in the insufficient reach of the tradition, arguing that more work needs to be done on it, and that, however extensive it seems to us, it is still inadequate, and centuries will have to pass before it is sufficiently established. The only bright spot in this otherwise discouraging schema is the belief that one day a time will come when tradition and its study will breathe a sigh of relief and reach a conclusion, when everything will have been made clear—that the law is the property of the people—and then the nobility will disappear. This is not said with any animus towards the nobility—not at all and not by anyone—we would rather hate ourselves because we are not yet worthy of the law. And that is why this, on the face of it, very attractive party, which believes in no law as such, has remained so small, because it also completely recognizes the nobility and its right to exist. It is really only possible to express this in a kind of self-contradiction: a party that would reject the nobility as well as the belief in the laws would straightaway have the entire population behind it, but such a party cannot come into being, because no one dares to reject the nobility. We live on the edge. An author once put it this way: the only visible unquestionable law that has been imposed on us is the nobility, and who are we to rob ourselves of the only law we have?

The Troop Levy

Troop levies—a neccessity in view of the constant violation of our frontiers—happen as follows:

Orders are given that on a certain day in a certain part
of town, all the inhabitants—men, women, and children
alike—are to remain at home. As a rule, some time toward
midday, the young nobleman who is to conduct the levy appears in the part of town where a detachment of soldiers, in-
fantry, and cavalry have been waiting since early morning.
He is a young man, slender, not tall, frail, casually dressed,
with tired eyes, racked with anxiety like an invalid with shiv-
ering fits. Without looking at anyone, he makes a sign with
the whip that is the only thing he carries, and a handful of soldiers fall in with him when he walks into the first building.
A soldier who knows all the inhabitants personally reads out
the list of names. Generally, all are present, standing there
in a line in the best room, their eyes fixed on the nobleman,
as though they were soldiers already. But it can also happen
that one or two, always a man or men, are missing. No one
dares to come up with an excuse, much less a lie; everyone
is silent, they can barely withstand the pressure of the order which someone in the house has violated, but the silent
presence of the nobleman holds them all in place. The noble-

man gives a signal, not even a nod of the head, it's just there in his eyes, and two soldiers go off to look for the missing person. It's not at all difficult. He's never actually gone from the building, nor does he really mean to absent himself from his service, it's only out of fear that he hasn't presented himself, fear not of the service itself, but shyness of it, the order is too vast, too frighteningly great for him, he can't comply with it voluntarily. Nor has he fled, he's merely hidden himself, and when he hears that the nobleman is in the building, then in all probability he creeps out of his hiding place to the door of the room, and is seized by the soldiers the moment they step outside. He is brought before the nobleman who clutches his whip in both hands—he is so feeble, he could do nothing at all with one hand—and beats the man. It won't have hurt him much, because half in exhaustion, half in disgust, he drops his whip, and the man has to pick it up and return it to him. Only then is he permitted to step back into the line of those waiting; incidentally, it is almost certain that he will not be taken. There are also times—and this actually happens more frequently—when there are more people present than appear on the list. A girl is there, for instance, and she stares at the nobleman; she is from somewhere else, the provinces somewhere, the levy has brought her here; there are many women who are unable to resist the lure of such a levy in some other place—it has a different character than at home. And strangely, there is nothing culpable about a woman giving into this temptation; on the contrary, it is something that in some people's opinion women need to go through—an obligation, something they owe to their gender. It always happens the same way. The girl or woman gets to hear that a levy is happening somewhere, perhaps very far away, with relatives or friends. She asks her family for permission to travel, they give their consent—they can hardly refuse—she puts on her best dress, she's more cheerful than normal, and calm and friendly at the same time, indifferent as she may be the rest of the time, and behind all the friendliness and the calm she is inaccessible as a complete stranger who is going home now and has nothing else on her mind. The family where the levy is taking place welcomes her quite unlike a normal guest: everything is done to flatter her, she is shown around all the rooms of the house, leans out of all the windows and if she happens to lay her hand on someone's head, it signifies more than a father's blessing. When the family gets ready for the levy, she is given the best seat, which is the one beside the door where she will have the best view of the nobleman and will best be seen by him. She is honored, but only until the nobleman enters; thereafter she positively withers. He looks at her as little as he looks at anyone else, and even if he happens to direct his gaze at someone, that person will not feel as if they've been seen. She wasn't expecting that, or rather that was exactly what she had been expecting, because it can happen no other way, but it wasn't the expectation of the contrary that led her to come here, it was just something that is now at an end. She feels shame to a degree that our own women perhaps never feel, only now does it dawn on her that she has forced her way into a levy belonging to others, and when the soldier has read out the list and her name didn't occur, there is a brief moment of silence, and she flees trembling and bowed out of the door, and is sent on her way by a blow on the back from the soldier.

If there is a man over, then he will want nothing but to be taken in the levy, even if it's not his house. That too is completely hopeless, as no such supernumerary has ever been conscripted, nor will anything of the kind ever happen.

Poseidon

Poseidon was sitting at his desk working. The administration of all the waters was a huge task. He could have had as many assistants as he wanted, and in fact he did have a large staff, but since he took his job very seriously and checked all the calculations himself, assistants were of little use to him. One couldn't say that the work made him happy either; he only did it because it was his to do. Yes, he had often requested happier work, as he put it, but whenever they came back to him with suggestions, it turned out that nothing appealed to him. It was actually very difficult to find anything else for him. It was hardly possible to put him in charge of a particular sea, quite apart from the fact that the calculations involved were just as onerous, only on a lesser scale of magnitude, since great Poseidon was only ever in line for a senior executive post. And if he was offered a job with a different department, the very thought of it was enough to turn his stomach, his divine breath became restless, his bronze thorax quaked. Not that they took his complaints all that seriously: if a great power kicks up, then you have to be seen to give into him, even in the most hopeless cause; no one seriously thought of having Poseidon removed from office, he had been god of the seas from the beginning of time, and would have to remain such.

The thing that most angered him—and this was the principal cause of his unhappiness in his job—was when he got to hear what people thought it involved, that is, forever parting the waves with his trident. And when all the time he was sitting at the bottom of the ocean up to his ears in figures, the occasional visit to Jupiter was really the only break in the monotony; a visit, moreover, from which he usually returned in a towering bad temper. He saw very little of the seas, only fleetingly on his hurried way up to Olympus, and he had never sailed them as such. He tended to say he was waiting for the world to end first, because there was bound to be a quiet moment when he had signed off on his last calculation and would be able to take himself on a little cruise somewhere.

Friendship

We are five friends who once emerged from a house one after the other; first one of us came out and stood beside the gate, then the second, or rather he slipped out of the gate as easily as a ball of mercury, and came to a stop next to the first, then the third, the fourth, the fifth. Finally we were all standing there in a row. People noticed us, pointed to us and said: Look, those five men have just come out of that building. Since that time we've been living together, and it would have been a peaceful life if it hadn't been for the efforts of a sixth to get involved all the time. He doesn't do anything, but he irritates us, and that's enough; why try to impose on us when we don't want him? We don't know him, and we don't want to include him. The five of us didn't know each other before and, if you like, we don't really know each other now, but what is possible and tolerated among the five of us is not possible and not tolerated with a sixth. Besides, we're five, and we don't want to be six. And what's this continual being together in aid of anyway? Even with the five of us it's pointless, though now we're together and we're staying together—but we don't want a further union, simply on the basis of our experiences together. But how to tell that to the sixth—giving long explanations would be almost like adopting him into our group, so we prefer not to explain anything, and just not to adopt him. Never mind how much he pouts, we push him away with our elbows; but never mind how much we push him away, he keeps coming back.

Our City Coat of Arms

At first, everything to do with the Tower of Babel was in good order, yes, perhaps even too good, and excessive attention was paid to signposts, interpreters, workers' lodgings, and supply roads, as though centuries of work lay ahead. The prevailing orthodoxy was that it was impossible to work too slowly; it wasn't even necessary to exaggerate this view, and one could still shrink back in alarm from laying the foundations. The argument ran like this: the kernel of this whole enterprise is the thought of building a tower that will reach into heaven. Next to this thought, everything else is negligible. This thought, once entertained in its full scope, is incapable of disappearing; as long as there are people in the world, there will be a strong desire to complete the tower. In this respect, then, one needs have little concern for the future; on the contrary, human knowledge will grow, the art of building has made progress and will make more; a job that may take us a year, in a hundred years' time may only take six months, and be better, moreover, more durable. So why work at the limits of our endurance already? That would only make sense if we could hope to build the tower in the space of a single generation. But that was not to be

expected. Rather, we might think that the following generation, with their improved knowledge, would find fault with
the work of their predecessors, and have the structure torn
down, to begin again. Such thoughts paralyzed us, so that,
more than with the tower itself, people busied themselves
with the building of the workers' city. Every national crew
wanted to have the most splendid quarters, and the upshot
was quarrels that were exacerbated into bloody conflicts.
These conflicts were unending; for the leaders they were a
further argument that the tower should be built either very
slowly, because of our poor concentration, or preferably only
following the return of peace. But people did not just spend
the time fighting: in the intervals they beautified the town,
which only provoked fresh envy and fresh conflicts. So the
first generation passed, but none of those following was any
different—craftsmanship improved but with that came the
desire to fight.

A further factor was that by the second or third generation the futility of the infinite tower was seen, but everyone
had become too committed to it to leave the town. Everything the town has produced by way of legends and songs is
informed by a yearning for a prophesied day on which the
town will be shattered by a giant fist in five quick consecu-
tive blows. That is why the city has a mailed fist on its coat
of arms.

The Helmsman

Am I not the helmsman?" I called out. "You?" asked a tall dark man, rubbing his eyes as though to dispel a dream. I had stood by the wheel in the dark night, with the feebly burning lantern over my head, and now this fellow had turned up and was trying to push me aside. And since I wouldn't yield, he put his foot on my chest and slowly pushed me down, while I clung to the spokes of the wheel and, as I slid to the ground, pulled the wheel right round. Then the man grabbed hold of it, straightened the course, and pushed me away. But I thought quickly, ran to the passageway that led down to the mess room and called out: "Shipmates! Comrades! Quick! A stranger has got me away from the wheel!" Slowly they came, climbing the steps—staggering, tired, mighty forms. "Am I not the helmsman?" I asked. They nodded, but only had eyes for the stranger. They stood around him in a half circle, and when he ordered "Get out of my way," they grouped together, nodded to me and went back down the stairs. Those people! Do they ever think, or do they just shuffle stupidly across the planet?

Consolidation

There were five of us in the business: the bookkeeper, who was a shortsighted melancholy man spread out across the ledger like a frog, quiet, but rising and falling feebly with his labored breathing; then the clerk, a little man with a gymnast's broad chest, who could set one hand down on the desk and vault over it in a light and elegant arc, only his face remaining serious as he looked around. Then we had a sales assistant, an old maid, slender and delicate, in a close-fitting dress; generally she kept her head to one side and smiled with her thin, wide lips. I, the trainee, who had little to do but hang around the desk with my duster, often felt like taking her hand—a long, weak, desiccated, wood-colored hand—as it lay casually or absentmindedly on her desk, and stroking it or kissing it or even—and this would have been the summit of bliss—resting my face where it felt so good, and only now and again changing my position, so that there might be justice and each cheek could get its turn. But this never happened; instead, as I approached, she would stretch out her hand and point me to some new task, somewhere in some distant corner, or at the top of the ladder. This last was particularly unwelcome to me, because the top of the room was terribly hot from the open gas flames which we used for lighting; nor was I free from vertigo, and I often felt sick up there. Sometimes, under the pretext of especially thorough cleaning, I would rest my head on a shelf and briefly cry, or, if nobody was watching, I would complain silently to the old maid down below. I knew that she didn't have any executive power, here or elsewhere, but I somehow thought she could have such power if she wanted, and use it for my advantage. But she didn't want, she didn't even use such power as she did have. She was, for instance, the only one of us whom the undermanager would occasionally obey. Apart from her, he was the most stiff-necked among us, of course he was the oldest as well, he had worked for the previous boss, he had done a lot of things here that we others had no idea of, but from all that he drew the wrong conclusion, which was that he had a better grasp of the business than anyone else, that not only could he keep the books much better than the bookkeeper, for example, or serve the customers better than the clerk, and so on and so forth, and that he had taken on the position of dogsbody freely, because no one else, not even an incapable person, could have been found to fill it. And so he tormented himself, though he was probably never very strong to begin with; and now had become a certified wreck, having been lumbered for the past forty years with the hand cart, the boxes, and the parcels. He had taken on the role voluntarily, but people had forgotten that: times had changed, he was no longer recognized, and while all around him in the business the most grotesque mistakes were made, he was not allowed to jump in, but had to choke down his despair, and remain chained to his arduous tasks.

The Test

I am a servant, but there is no work for me. I am timid and unpushy, I don't even cut in line, but that's just one cause of my idleness, quite possibly it has nothing whatever to do with my idleness, the main cause of which is that I feel no vocation to serve. Others have a calling and haven't applied any harder than I did; yes, perhaps they didn't even have the desire to have a calling, whereas I sometimes have it very strongly.

So I lie on my pallet in the servants' quarters, looking up at the beams, fall asleep, wake up, fall asleep again. Sometimes I cross the road to the pub where they serve you sour beer; it's so disgusting sometimes that I've poured it down the drain, but then I go back to drinking it later. I like being there because I can sit at the little closed window and look across at the windows of our house without anyone seeing me. There's not much to see on the street side, I think, only the corridor windows, and not even the corridors in the master's apartments. I may be wrong, but someone once claimed that was the case, without my even asking him, and my general sense of the layout seems to bear it out. It's rare for a window to be opened, and when it does happen, it's one of the servants doing it, and then he leans on the sill and looks out for a while. So there are corridors where you're safe from surprise. By the way, I don't know any of those servants— the servants who work upstairs sleep somewhere else, not in my quarters.

One time, when I came to the pub, I found someone sitting in my place. I didn't dare look closely at him, and felt like turning round and leaving. But he called me over, and it turned out he was a servant too, whom I had seen somewhere once, though we had never spoken. "Why are you running away? Sit down and have a drink. My treat." So I sat down. He asked me this and that, but I couldn't give him any answers; I couldn't even understand his questions. So I said: "Maybe you're regretting having asked me to sit with you. I'd better go," and stood up. But he put out his hand across the table, and pulled me down: "Stay here," he said, "that was just a test. Whoever doesn't answer the questions has passed the test."

The Vulture

There was a vulture that hacked at my feet. He had already shredded my boots and my socks, now he was attacking my feet. He picked away at them, then he flew around me a couple of times skittishly, before resuming his work. A gentleman came along and watched for a while, then he asked me why I tolerated the vulture. "I'm helpless," I said. "He came and started hacking at me, and of course I wanted to drive him away, I even tried to throttle him, but a beast like that has a lot of strength in him, and he was about to leap at my face, so I thought it was better to sacrifice my feet. Now they're almost shredded." "How can you stand to be tormented like that," said the gentleman, "a single bullet, and that vulture is history." "Is that right?" I asked, "and would you oblige me?" "Willingly," said the gentleman, "I just have to go home and get my gun. Can you wait another half an hour?" "I don't know," I said, and I stood for a while, rigid with pain. Then I said: "Well, will you try anyway?" "Very well," said the gentleman, "I'll be as quick as I can."

The vulture had been listening to our conversation, and kept looking back and forth between me and the gentleman. Now I saw that he had understood everything. He flew up, leaning right back to get plenty of momentum, and then, like a javelin thrower, he thrust his beak through my mouth deep into me. As I fell back, I could feel a sense of deliverance as he wallowed and drowned in the blood that now filled all my vessels and burst its banks.

Little Fable

Oh," said the mouse, "the world gets narrower with each passing day. It used to be so wide that I was terrified, and I ran on and felt happy when at last I could see walls in the distance to either side of me—but these long walls are converging so quickly that already I'm in the last room and there in the corner is the trap I'm running into." "You only have to change your direction," said the cat, and ate it up.

The Spinning Top

A philosopher liked to be among children who were playing. When he saw a boy with a spinning top, it would set him on edge. No sooner was the top spinning than the philosopher would set off after it to catch it. He didn't care that the children shouted and tried to keep him away from their toy; if he managed to catch the top while it was still spinning, he was happy—though only for a moment—then he would throw it down on the ground and walk off. He believed that the understanding of any little thing, for instance of a spinning top, enabled one to understand everything. Therefore he never worried his head about big problems—that struck him as inefficient; if the least triviality was thoroughly explored, then everything was understood, and so he occupied himself only with the spinning top. And each time preparations had been made for spinning the top, he hoped this time he would be successful, and then the top started spinning and in his breathless pursuit of it his hope became a certainty, but then when he held the stupid piece of wood in his hand, he felt ill, and the shouting of the children which he hadn't been aware of thus far, chased him off, and he went reeling on his way like a top himself, being lashed by a clumsy whip.

The Departure

I gave orders for my horse to be fetched. The servant didn't understand me. I went to the stables myself, saddled my horse, and got on it. In the distance I could hear a trumpet. I asked him what that meant. He didn't know, and hadn't heard it. At the gate he stopped me and asked: "And where are you going, sir?" "I don't know," I said, "away from here, away from here. Only if I keep going away from here, can I reach my destination." "So you know your destination?" he asked. "Yes," I said. "I told you already, it's 'away-from-here,' that's where I'm going." "You don't have any provisions with you," he said. "I don't need any," I said, "the journey is so long that I will certainly starve if I don't find something to eat on the way. No provisions can save me. Luckily, this is a truly enormous journey."

Advocates

It was very doubtful whether I had any advocates. I was unable to discover any exact information, the faces all looked discouraging, most of the people who came up to me and whom I saw repeatedly in the corridors looked like fat old women—they were wearing large blue-and-white-striped aprons that covered their entire body, they stroked their bellies, and turned cumbersomely this way and that. I couldn't even establish if we were in a court building or not. Some things suggested yes; many others no. More than any details, there was a kind of far-off droning noise all the time that reminded me most strongly of a court. I couldn't tell where it was coming from, it filled all the rooms to such a degree that you could assume it came from everywhere, or perhaps the place where I happened to be was the site of this droning sound, but that was certainly not the case, because it also seemed to be coming from far away. These corridors, narrow, arched and slowly turning, with austerely decorated lintels, seemed to have been constructed for profound silence—these were corridors fit for a museum or a library.

But if it wasn't a court, what was I doing looking for an

advocate here? Because I was looking for an advocate everywhere, I need one everywhere, if anything you need one
less in a court of law than elsewhere, because the court will
speak its judgment according to the law. If you thought it
did so without regard to justice or responsibility, then life
would be impossible. You need to trust the court to give
free play to the majesty of the law, because that is its only
function, but in the law, everything is accusation, plea, and
judgment—the gratuitous involvement of an individual here
would be a desecration. It's a different matter with the facts
of a judgment, these are based on inquiries—inquiries here
and there—with family and strangers, with friends and enemies, with relatives and *coram publico*, in the city and the
village—in a word, everywhere. Here it is urgently necessary to have advocates—advocates in numbers, ideally advocates in serried ranks, a living wall of them, because by
their nature advocates are unwieldy, whereas the prosecutors, those wily foxes, those nippy weasels, those invisible
voles slip through the smallest crannies and whisk through
between the feet of the advocates. So be careful! That's why
I'm here, I'm collecting advocates. But I haven't found any
yet, just these old women who keep coming and going; if I
weren't here looking, it would put me to sleep. I am not in
the right place, and unfortunately I can't resist the conclusion that I am not in the right place. I should be in a place
where people come together from all strata, from all professions, various ages. I should have the chance to pick out
from the crowd the kindliest, best qualified ones who will
keep an eye out for me. The best place to recruit might be a
large fairground. Instead, I drift up and down these corridors,
where there are just these old women and not too many of
them either, and always the same ones. Even those few, in

spite of their slowness, won't permit themselves to be confronted by me, they slip away from me, they float like rain clouds, they are wholly taken up with unknown occupations. Why do I so blindly rush into a building, not reading the inscription over the gate, am straightaway in the corridors, sitting here so obstinately that I can't remember ever having been outside, ever having run up a flight of stairs.

But I can't go back—the waste of time, the acknowledgement of a mistake, would be unendurable. How in this short, hasty life, accompanied by an impatient droning sound, can I run down a flight of stairs? Not possible. The time allotted you is so short that if you lose a second, you have lost the whole of your life, because there is no more of it than that; it's only as long as the time you're wasting. So when you've set out on your way, pursue it, come what may, you can only win, you don't run any risk. Maybe you will fall down in the end, but if you had retraced your steps after the first few paces, and had gone back down the stairs, then you would have fallen right at the outset, and not as a possibility, but as a certainty. So if you don't find anything in the corridors, open the doors; if you find nothing behind the doors, there are more stories; if you find nothing upstairs, never mind, swing yourself up more flights of stairs—as long as you don't stop climbing, the steps won't stop; under your climbing feet they grow upward.

In Our Synagogue . . .

In our synagogue lives an animal about the size of a marten. There have been many sightings of it, as it will allow a human being to approach to within five feet. Its color is a pale turquoise. No one has yet touched its fur, so there is nothing to be said about that, although one would like to insist that its true color is unknown and that the color one sees is as a result of the dust and mortar that have caught in its fur, the color bearing some resemblance to the inside of the synagogue, only a little lighter. Aside from its timidity, it is an unusually calm and sessile animal; if it weren't scared so often, it would probably move around less. Its preferred spot is the grille overlooking the women's section. There, with visible glee, it hooks itself fast to the metalwork, stretches out and looks down into the prayer room; its exposed position seems to give it pleasure, but the temple servant is under instructions not to permit the animal by the grille, otherwise it would get used to the spot, and that can't be allowed to happen because the women are afraid of the animal. Why they should be afraid of it is a little unclear. At first sight it can look fearsome—the long neck, the triangular face, the almost horizontally protuberant teeth, on the upper lip a line of long—longer than the teeth—evidently very spiny pale bristles, all of which can indeed give one a turn, but soon one will understand how harmless this apparent terror actually is. Above all, it steers clear of people, it's shyer than a forest animal, its ties are exclusively to the building, and its tragedy lies in the fact that the building it has chosen is a synagogue, which at times can be a very animated place. If communication with the animal had been possible, then we would have been able to offer it the assurance that the community in our little highland town is shrinking by the year, and is already having difficulties finding the funds to keep up the building. It is quite possible that in a while our synagogue will have become a granary or something of the sort, and that the animal will find the peace it so painfully lacks now.

It is only our women who are afraid of the animal—the men have long since become indifferent to it—one generation has shown it to the next, it has been seen time and time again; in the end we don't even raise our eyes to look at it, and even the children, seeing it for the first time, no longer remark on it. It has become the synagogue pet, and why should the synagogue not have a special pet that doesn't appear anywhere else? If it weren't for the women, we should hardly be aware of the existence of the beast. But even the women are not really afraid of it: it would be too odd as well, to fear an animal like that, day in, day out, for years, for decades. They say in their defense that the animal is usually closer to them than it is to the men, and this is true. The animal doesn't dare go down to the men, and no one has ever seen it on the floor. If it is banished from the grille to the women's section, then it tries to keep the same elevation on the opposite wall. There is a very narrow ledge there, barely two fingers' breadth; it runs around three sides of the synagogue, and on this ledge the animal sometimes dashes back and forth; usually, though, it sits quietly in a particular spot overlooking the women.

It's almost inexplicable how it can use this narrow path so easily, and the way it turns, having reached the end, is quite remarkable. It is already a very old animal, but it never hesitates to perform the most daring somersault, which never fails either: it turns around in midair, and there it is doubling back again the same way. Admittedly, if you've seen it a few times, you've probably seen it enough and you've no need to see it again. It's neither fear nor curiosity that keeps the women agitated; if they worked harder at their praying, they could forget all about the animal, as the devout women do, if only the others who are in the majority would allow it, but they like to draw attention to themselves, and the animal is a welcome pretext for doing so. If they could, and if they dared, they would have lured the animal even closer to themselves, in order to show still more fear of it. But in reality, it's not their proximity that the animal seeks; as long as it's not being attacked, it's every bit as indifferent to them as it is to the men; ideally it would probably remain in the obscurity in which it lives when there are no prayers—evidently in some hole in the wall that we have yet to discover. It's only when we start to pray that it appears; alarmed by the noise, it wants to see what's going on, it wants to remain alert, to be free, capable of flight; fear causes it to emerge, fear causes it to perform its somersaults, and then it doesn't dare retreat until the service is over. It quite naturally prefers its elevation because there it has security and the best possibilities of running on grille or ledge, but it's not always there by any means, sometimes it climbs down toward the men—the curtain of the Ark is held by a gleaming brass rail that seems to tempt the animal, often it has been seen creeping toward it, but then it always sits there quietly. Even when it's sitting just behind the Ark, you couldn't say it was being disruptive, with its shiny, always open, possibly lidless eyes that seem to gaze at the congregation, without regarding anyone in particular, just looking in the direction of the dangers from which it may feel threatened.

In this respect, until recently at least, it seemed not much less understanding than our women. What dangers does it have to fear? Who intends it any harm? And hasn't it lived for many years in a completely self-contained way? The men aren't bothered by its presence, and the majority of the women would probably be disappointed if it disappeared. And since it's the only animal in the building, it hasn't any natural enemies. It could have seen that over the course of the years. And while the religious service with all its noise may be very alarming to the animal, it is replayed day after day in a moderate way, heightened on the holy days, but always regularly and without interruption. Even the most timid animal should have been able to get used to it by now, particularly if it saw that it's not the sound of pursuers, but a noise that doesn't concern it at all. And still the fear. Is it the memory of times long gone, or a presentiment of times to come? Does this old animal perhaps know more than the three generations that foregather in the synagogue each time?

Many years ago, apparently, attempts were made to drive the animal away. Perhaps they were, but more likely it's just a story. What can be confirmed, though, is that we made inquiries whether it was permissible, from the point of view of religious law, to tolerate such an animal in the house of God. Views from various prominent rabbis were solicited, opinions differed, the majority were in favor of expulsion and the reconsecration of the house of God, but that was more easily said than done—in reality it was impossible to drive the animal away.

Once Upon a Time There Was a Game ...

Once upon a time there was a game of patience and dexterity, not much bigger than a pocket watch, and without any sensational innovations. Various grooves had been etched in blue in the russet-colored wooden surface, culminating in a small hollow. The ball, which was also blue, was by angling and shaking to be got first into one of the grooves and then ultimately into the hollow. Once the ball was in the hollow, the game was over, and if you wanted to play it again, you merely had to give the toy a shake. The whole thing was covered by a stout piece of convex glass; you could keep the game in your pocket and carry it with you wherever you were going, and could take it out at will and play it.

When the ball was otherwise unengaged, it mostly wandered about, with its hands behind its back, over the high ground, avoiding the paths. It was of the view that it was sufficiently tormented by the paths when the game was in progress, and it had rights, during such time as it wasn't, to recreate itself on the open plains. It had rather a rolling gait, and claimed it wasn't really well suited to the narrow paths. This was partially true, it did indeed have trouble gripping the paths, but it was also untrue, because in fact it was very carefully adapted to the breadth of the paths, though they weren't to be too comfortable, because then the game would have involved little patience and no dexterity.

Investigations of a Dog

How my life has changed, and in other ways, hardly at all! When I remember the times when I was still living in the midst of dogs, taking part in everything that concerned them—a dog among dogs—I do find on closer examination that there was always something not quite right about the picture, a little breach or rupture; a mild unease would befall me at the heart of the most respected tribal occasions, yes, sometimes even in intimate settings; no, not just sometimes, but very often, the sight of a dear fellow dog, his mere aspect, somehow seen afresh, could make me embarrassed, shocked, alarmed—yes, even desperate. I tried to calm myself, friends I discussed it with helped me, quieter times came along, times that were not free of such surprises either, only they were accepted in a spirit of greater equanimity, were more casually absorbed into the tissue of life; perhaps they made me sad and tired, but they allowed me to continue to exist as a perhaps somewhat aloof, reserved, frightened, calculating, but all in all regulation dog. How—without these pauses for refreshment—could I ever have reached my proud age; how could I have forced my way through to the calm with which I observe the terrors of my youth and bear the terrors of my seniority; how could I ever have learned to draw the correct conclusions from my admittedly unhappy or, putting it more cautiously, not so terribly happy constitution and live almost entirely by their light? Withdrawn, solitary, entirely taken up with my small, hopeless but—to me—indispensable inquiries, that's how I live, but in so doing I never lost sight of my people from a distance, often news of them reached me, and from time to time I let them hear of my doings. I am treated with respect—they don't understand my way of living, but they don't hold it against me and even young dogs I see running by in the distance from time to time, a new generation, whose infancy I can barely recall, do not deny me a respectful greeting.

It would be wrong to suppose that, for all my—all too apparent—eccentricities, I have completely lost touch with the species. If I think about it, and I have the time and inclination and capacity to do so, we dogs are an odd lot. Apart from ourselves, there are many other creatures round about—poor, inadequate, mute beings, restricted to the odd squawk at best—we have studied them, given them names, tried to help them along, to ennoble them, and so on and so forth, but to me, so long as they don't bother me, they are a matter of indifference. I get them mixed up or ignore them, but one thing remains too striking for me ever to forget it, and that is how little, compared to us dogs, they consort, how they pass by one another like strangers, how they have neither high nor low interests in common, how on the contrary any interests they have seem to drive them further apart than they already are. Whereas we dogs! One may surely say that we live in a pack, all of us, however different we may be in terms of the innumerable and profound distinctions that have arisen between us over the ages. All one pack! We are impelled to be together, and nothing can prevent us from satisfying that urge; all our laws and institutions, the few I still know, and the numberless ones I have forgotten, they all go back to the greatest happiness that exists for us, our warm companionableness. And now the obverse. No creature to the best of my knowledge lives in such a dispersed way as we dogs, none has so many, so impossibly many differences of kind, of breed, of occupation. We, who want to be together—and repeatedly we are able to, at moments of exaltation—we of all creatures live remote from one another, in curious callings, which are often hard for the dog next door to understand, clinging to regulations that are not of our making—yes, that seem, if anything, to be directed against us. These are such difficult matters, matters one would prefer not to interfere with—I understand such a point of view, understand it better than my own—and yet I have allowed them to govern my life. Why do I not do as others do, live in harmony with my people, and accept in silence what disturbs the harmony, ignore it like a small error in a large reckoning, and keep my eye on the thing that links us happily together, not that which repeatedly and irresistibly rips us out of our community. . . .

I remember an incident from my youth. I was in one of those inexplicable states of blissful excitement that we probably all experience as children—I was still a very young dog, liking everything, attached to everything. I believed that great things were happening around me, whose focus I was, to which I needed to lend my voice, things that would be condemned to lie languishing on the ground if I didn't run on their behalf, swing my body around for them—childish fantasies that recede over the years, but at that time they were very strong, I was wholly in thrall to them—and then something quite extraordinary happened, which seemed to confirm these wild expectations of mine. Intrinsically it was nothing extraordinary, and later on I saw such things, and others, still stranger, quite regularly, but at the time it struck me with a primal, powerful, indelible impression that set the tone for much that followed. I encountered a small group of dogs, or rather I didn't encounter them, they approached me. I had then been running around for a long time in the dark, with a presentiment of great things, a presentiment that was a little misleading admittedly, because it was always with me. I had long been running through the darkness, this way and that, guided by nothing but a vague yearning, then suddenly I stopped with the sense that I was in the right place, I looked up, and it was a full dazzling day, with just a little heat-haze. I greeted the morning with confused sounds, then—just as if I had summoned them—from some darkness there emerged into the light with grotesque noise the like of which I had never heard, seven dogs. Had I not clearly seen that they were dogs, and that they were accompanied by their noise—though I was unable to see quite how they managed to produce it—I would have run off; but as it was, I stayed put.

At that time I understood almost nothing about the musicality exclusive to our species, it had managed to escape my burgeoning attention so far; there had been vague attempts to point me toward it, nothing more, and so much the more astonishing, yes, positively overwhelming was the impression made on me by these seven artistes. They didn't speak, they didn't sing, they tended to silence almost with a certain—forgive me—doggedness, but from empty space they contrived to conjure up music. All was music. The picking up and setting down of their feet, certain anglings of

the head, their running and resting, the positions they took
relative to one another, the recurring associations they entered with one another, with one, say, resting his forepaws
on another's back, and then all seven performing this same
action, so that the first bore the weight of all the others,
or the way their bodies creeping low to the ground made
tangled forms—never erring, not even the last of them who
was still a little unsure of himself and didn't straightaway
find the connection to those ahead of him, so to speak, in
striking the tune, sometimes missed a cue, but that was
only by comparison to the great certainty of the others, and
even had his own relative uncertainty been far greater, a
complete uncertainty, it would not have managed to spoil
anything, while the others, the great masters, imperturbably
kept the beat. But then I hardly saw them, I could hardly
take them in. They had stepped forth. I had privately greeted
them as dogs, though of course I was greatly confused by
the sound that accompanied them, but they had to be dogs,
dogs like me and you. I looked at them through the eyes
of habit, like dogs one might meet on the street. I felt like
approaching them, for an exchange of greetings: they were
very near to me, dogs a lot older than I was and not of my
longhaired woolly kind, but nor were they that alien to me
either in form and stature—they seemed somehow familiar,
I knew many of their sort or similar sorts, but while I was
still caught up in these reflections, the music gradually took
over, veritably taking possession of me, pulling me away
from these actual little dogs, quite against my will; in fact,
while I was resisting it with all my might, howling like a
dog in pain, I was permitted to occupy myself with nothing
else but the music that came at me from all sides—from
the heights, from the depths, from everywhere, taking the

listener in its midst, flooding him, crushing him, even as he was annihilated, in such proximity that it felt remote, like barely audible fanfares in the distance. And then I was let go, because I was too exhausted, too destroyed, too weak to be able to hear; I was released, and I saw seven little dogs in a procession, doing their leaps. I felt like calling out to them, however disdainful they looked, to ask them for a lesson, ask them what they were doing here—I was a child after all, and thought I had a right to put my questions to all and sundry—but no sooner had I begun, no sooner had I felt the good familiar doggish connection with the seven than the music returned and drove me wild. I walked around in small circles, as though I myself was one of the musicians, whereas I was only their victim, flung myself this way and that, begging for mercy, and finally saved myself from its power only because it had forced me against a tangle of boards that seemed to have risen up in that place, without my having noticed it before, and now I was caught fast in it, it pressed my head down and, while the music was still thundering on in the open, made it possible for me to pause and catch my breath.

Truly, though, more than the artistry of the seven dogs—which was baffling to me, but also wholly impossible to account for, so totally beyond anything I knew—I was surprised at their courage in giving themselves over so wholly and openly to what they were producing, and at their strength to bear it so calmly, without it breaking their backs. I now began to see, on closer inspection from my little vantage point, that it wasn't so much calm as intense concentration with which they were working. Those apparently so securely stepping feet were in a continual fearful tremor; they looked at each other seemingly rigid with despair, and their tongues, which they made constant efforts to control, would then hang slackly from their muzzles. It couldn't be doubt of success that came over them; anyone who dared such a thing, or was capable of creating work of that order, surely couldn't be afraid. What was there for them to fear? Who compelled them to do what they were doing?

I was unable to restrain myself any longer, particularly once they seemed to me quite bafflingly in need of help, and so through all the noise I called out my questions loudly and peremptorily. They, though—baffling, baffling!—made no reply and ignored me, a breach of manners that under no circumstances is allowed the smallest or the greatest dog. So were they not dogs after all? But how could they not be dogs? Now, as I listened more closely, I heard the quiet words of encouragement they called to one another, pointing out difficulties ahead, warning each other of mistakes. I saw the least little dog, who was receiving the most calls, often squint in my direction, as though he wanted very badly to answer me, but was forcing himself not to, because he wasn't allowed. But why was it not allowed, how could the very thing that our laws unconditionally demand on this occasion not be permitted? My heart was outraged; I all but forgot the music. These dogs were in breach of the law. Great and magical artists they might be, but the law applied just as much to them, even as a child I understood that. And from then on I observed more and more. They really had good reason to be silent, assuming they were silent out of guilt. Because in the way they were carrying on—the music had blinded me to it so far—they had left all modesty behind: the wretches were doing the most ridiculous and obscene thing, they were walking upright on their hind legs. Faugh! They bared themselves, and exposed their nakedness to full view; they were proud of themselves and if they once obeyed a better impulse and dropped down onto their front legs, they positively shrank as though that had been a mistake, as though the whole of Nature was a mistake, and quickly lifted up their feet again. Their expression seemed to be asking forgiveness for briefly having interrupted their sinfulness.

Was the world out of kilter? Where was I? What had happened? At this point, for the sake of my own being, I could no longer hesitate. I freed myself from the embrace of the planks, leapt out with a single bound and made for the dogs—I, a little pupil, was called upon to be a teacher. I had to make them understand what they were doing, and keep them from further sin. "Such old dogs, such old dogs!" I kept tutting away to myself. But no sooner was I free, and there were just two or three paces between me and them, there was the noise again, reasserting its sway over me. Perhaps in my zeal I could have overcome it this time, since I knew it better now, had it not been for the fact that in all its terrible but still resistible polyphony, a clear, stern, constant, and unvarying tone was coming at me from ever so far away— perhaps it was the actual melody in the midst of the noise— that forced me to my knees. Oh, what beguiling music these dogs could make. I couldn't go on, I no longer wanted to lecture them; let them sprawl with their feet apart, commit sins and lead others to the sin of quiet spectating. I was such a small dog—who could demand something so difficult of me? I made myself even smaller than I was already, I whimpered, if the dogs had stopped and asked me for an opinion then, I might very well have agreed with them. In any case, it didn't go on for very much longer, and they disappeared with all their sound and light into the darkness from which they had sprung.

As I say, there was really nothing remarkable about the whole incident; in the course of a long life you will experience many things that, taken out of context and viewed through the eyes of a child, will be much more remarkable. And then, too, one can of course—as the expression goes—talk anything up. All that happened was that seven musicians had met to make music on a quiet morning, and a small dog had blundered upon them, an irritating spectator whom they tried, unfortunately in vain, to drive away by especially terrible or especially elevated music. If his questions were bothersome to them, were they, irked already by the mere presence of the stranger, to respond to this nuisance and add to it by providing answers? And even if the law instructs us to give answers to everyone, is such a tiny stray so-and-so even to be termed as anyone? Maybe they couldn't understand him; presumably he was lisping out his questions in a way that was hard to understand. Or perhaps they understood him perfectly well and mastered themselves to the extent of providing answers, but he, the little fellow, unused to music, couldn't tell the answers from the music. And as far as the business with the hind legs goes, maybe they really only walked like that on a few rare occasions. Yes, of course, it is a sin! But they were alone together—seven of them—a community of friends in the privacy of their own four walls, so to speak; quite alone, if you like, because to be among friends is not like being on public view, and then it takes more than the chance presence of a nosy little street dog to make an occasion public; therefore, is it not the case instead that nothing really happened? Not quite, perhaps, but very nearly, and the lesson is that parents should keep their little ones from running around so much, and train them to remain silent and respect their elders.

If that is indeed so, then the case is settled. Though settled for grown-ups doesn't settle it for the little ones. I was running around, telling people, asking questions, making accusations, investigating, and wanting to drag anyone at all off to the place where it had all happened, to show everyone where I had stood and where the seven had been and where and how they had danced and made music, and if anyone had been willing to go there with me, instead of shaking me off and laughing at me, then I would have been prepared to sacrifice my being without sin, and would have tried to get up on my hind legs, to make everything utterly clear. Well, people are hard on children, though in the end they tend to forgive them. It seems I have kept my childlike nature, even as I have grown into an old dog myself. And so I never stopped talking aloud about that incident, though I place less importance on it today, breaking it up into its component parts, trying it out on all and sundry without regard to the society in which I found myself, always thinking about the issue, bending the ears of others as my own were bent, only—and this was the major difference between us—I felt impelled to get to the bottom of it, so as to free my mind for the quiet satisfactions of day-to-day living. I have gone on applying myself, though with less childish means—the difference isn't as great as one might have expected—and yet even today I'm not much further along.

But it all began with that concert. I am not complaining, by the way, it's my inborn nature which, even if there had been no concert at all, would have found some other occasion to express itself. I only regretted the fact that it occurred so soon and took up such a lot of my childhood; the happy life of young dogs, that some are able to stretch out over many years, in my case was over in a matter of months.

Well, never mind! There are more important things than childhood. And perhaps old age, worked for over the course of a hard life, will offer me more in the way of childish happiness than an actual child would have the strength to endure, though I now will.

It was then that I embarked on my investigations. I wasn't short of material: rather, the excess of it drove me to distraction in my dark hours. I began to study what keeps us dogs nourished. Now, of course that's not a straightforward question; it's what's been preoccupying us from time immemorial. It is the main object of our research; a vast body of observations and theories and opinions has been assembled on the topic, it has become a science whose dimensions exceed the comprehension not just of any given individual, but of the totality of all scholars, and can finally only be borne by nothing less than the entirety of dogdom, and even then only partially and not without complaint; because bits of long-held historic knowledge are continually crumbling away, demanding to be painfully replaced, not to mention the complexities and the scarcely possible demands of integrating the new learning.

So don't come to me with this objection. I know all that at least as well as the dog on the street; it doesn't occur to me to consider what I do as in any way scientific, I am full of healthy respect for science, but to add to it I lack the understanding and the application and the peace of mind and—not least, especially over the last few years—the appetite. I gulp my food down as and when I find it, but don't consider it worth my while to subject it to any methodical agricultural examination. In this respect I am content to abide by the accepted distillation of all wisdom, the little rule with which the mother sends her pup from her dugs out into the wide world: "Wet everything as well as you can." And doesn't that indeed say pretty much everything? What has science, launched by our forebears, substantially to add to that? Details, details, and how uncertain all that is, whereas this rule will endure as long as dogs are dogs. It concerns our principal food; admittedly, we have other, auxiliary sources, but in general, and if times aren't too hard, then we can live from this principal source that we can find on the ground, while what the ground needs from us is our water, which nourishes it, and it is at that price that it gives us our food, whose production—lest it be forgotten—can be accelerated by certain invocations, songs, and ritual movements. But that really in my opinion is the sum total of everything that can usefully be said on the subject from this point of view. Here I am in full agreement with the great majority of dogdom, and I will have nothing to do with other views, which I consider to be heretical.

Truly, I am not concerned with special pleading or being proved right, I am happy to be in agreement with my fellows, and that is the case here. But my research leads me in another direction. I know from appearances that the earth, when sprinkled and worked according to all the rules of science, gives us nourishment in sufficient quantity and quality of such kinds, in such places, and at such times as accord with the principles partly or wholly established by science. I accept this, but my question remains: "From where does the earth take this food?" A question many claim not to understand, and to which at best the answer comes: "If you haven't got enough to eat, we'll give you some of ours." Mark this answer. I know that sharing individually obtained food with the generality is not among the strong points of the canine community. Life is hard, the earth is mean; science, so rich in understanding, is less so in practical outcomes; whoever has food will keep it; nor is that to be termed selfishness—it's the opposite, it's the law of the dog, a unanimous popular decision, proceeding from the overcoming of selfishness, because those in possession are always in the minority. Hence the reply, "If you haven't got enough to eat, we'll give you some of ours" is a joke, a tease, a *bon mot*. I have not forgotten that. But it had all the more significance for me because to me, going about the world with my questions, they left out the humorous aspect; I was still given nothing to eat—where would it have been obtained, in any case? And if someone just happened to have something, then of course, crazed with hunger as he was, any kind of compassionate regard was forgotten, but the offer was meant seriously and here and there I really did get the odd morsel, if I was quick enough to take possession of it. Why was it that others behaved so differently toward me? Favored me, spared me? Because I was a feeble scrawny dog, badly fed, and too little concerned with nourishing myself? But the world is full of badly fed dogs and we like to snatch even the worst food from their chops, if we can—not out of greed, but on principle.

No, I received preferential treatment, not to the extent that I could prove it in detail, but that certainly was my firm impression. So was it my questions that gave pleasure, that were taken to be particularly thoughtful? No, they gave no pleasure and some even thought they were stupid. And yet it could only be my questions that gained me their attention. It was as though they would rather do the extraordinary thing and stuff my mouth with food—they didn't do it, but they wanted to—than attend to my questions. But then they would have done better to chase me away, and have done with my questions that way. But no, they didn't want to do that, they might not have wanted to hear my questions, but they didn't want to chase me away just because of them either. It was as if, no matter how much I was laughed at, treated as a silly little animal, pushed this way and that, it was actually the time I was treated with the greatest respect; never again did anything similar happen to me; I was able to go everywhere, nothing was kept from me; under the pretext of brusqueness I was actually given kid-gloved treatment. And it had to be all on account of my questions, my impatience, my desire to investigate. Did they want to lull me, lead me off the false path without violence—almost lovingly—from a path whose wrongness wasn't so self-evident that it might have permitted the use of violence; in any case, a certain respect and fear may have kept them from violence. At the time I sensed something of the sort; today I know it much better than those who did it to me then: they did indeed want to divert me from my path. They weren't successful; they achieved the opposite and my attentiveness was heightened. I even had the impression that it was I who wanted to lead the others, and to some extent my attempt was successful. It was only with help from the dog community that I began to understand what my own questions were about. If I asked, for example, where does the earth get the food from, did I care, as it might have appeared that I did, about the earth and its concerns? Not in the least, as I soon discovered, that was furthest from my thoughts—all I cared about were the dogs, nothing else. For what is there apart from dogs? To whom else can one appeal in an otherwise empty world? All science, the totality of all questions and all answers, lies with us dogs. If only one could make this science productive, bring it to the light of day. If only they didn't know so infinitely more than they admit, even to themselves. The most garrulous dog is laconic by comparison with those places that offer the best food. You slink around your fellow dog, you froth with avidity, you lash yourself with your tail, you ask, you beg, you howl, you bite and finally you achieve—well, you achieve what you would have achieved without any exertion: a kindly hearing, friendly touches, respectful snufflings, intimate embraces, my and thy howls commingle—everything tends to make you find oblivion in delight. But the one thing you wanted above all to achieve—confirmation of what you know— that remains denied to you; to that request, whether tacit or voiced, if you have taken wheedling and tempting as far as they will go, you will be treated at best to blank expressions, dull, veiled eyes, looks askance.

It's not so very different from the way it was back then, in my youth, when I called out to the musician dogs and they were silent. Now you might say: "Here you are complaining about your fellow dogs and their silence on various crucial questions. You claim they know more than they're saying, more than they want to have said in their lives, and this silence, the reason and secret of which of course forms part of their silence, is poisoning your life, making it unendurable for you. You had to change it or quit it, maybe so, but aren't you a dog yourself, don't you have dog-knowledge? Well, tell us, not only in the form of a question, but as an answer. If you were to articulate it, who would be able to resist you? The great chorus of caninity would chime in with you, as if it had just been waiting for this moment. Then you would have truth, clarity, admission—as much as you wanted. The roof of the lowly life about which you have so many bad things to say will open, and we all, dog by dog, will rise through it into freedom and openness. And if the last should prove impossible, if it should all turn out to be worse than before, if the whole truth should be more unbearable than half the truth, if it should be confirmed that the silent ones are in the right because they are the sustainers of life, and should the slim hope we have now turn into utter helplessness, it will still have been worth the attempt, since you are unwilling to live as you are permitted to live. How can you hold their silence against others, and keep silent yourself?"

Easy answer: because I am a dog. Basically like the others, tight shut, offering resistance to my own questions, rigid with fear. Am I in fact, at least since I have become an adult, looking to dogdom for answers to my questions? Are my hopes so foolish? Do I see the foundations of our life, and sense their depth, watch the workers on the site, doing their grim work, and still expect that as far as my questions go, all that will be ended, torn down, abandoned? No, I really don't expect that any more. With my questions I am only chasing myself, driving myself on with the silence that is the only answer I get from all around me. How long do you think you can stand it that dogdom, which through your questions you are gradually bringing to consciousness, is silent and will always be silent? How long can you stand it: beyond all individual questions, that is the question of questions for my life; it's been put specifically to me, and troubles no one else. Unfortunately I can answer it more easily than the detailed, supplementary questions: I will presumably be able to stand it until my natural end—old age is placid and gets better and better at withstanding the restless questioning. I will probably die in silence, surrounded by silence, a peaceful death, and I am almost reconciled to it. An admirably strong heart and lungs not to be worn out ahead of time were given to us dogs almost out of malice, we resist all questions, even our own, being the wall of silence that we are.

More and more often of late, thinking about my life, I seek out the decisive and fundamental mistake I have probably committed—and can't find it. And yet I must have committed it, because if I hadn't and had still not attained what I wanted to attain, in spite of the honest endeavors of a long life, then it would have been proof that what I wanted was impossible, and the consequence would be utter hopelessness. Behold thy life's work! First of all, there were my investigations on the question: from where does the earth take our food. A young pup, avid for life, I renounced all pleasures, avoided all entertainments, when tempted I buried my head between my legs, and set to work. This was no scientific task, neither in terms of erudition, or method, or purpose. They were my mistakes, yes, but I don't suppose they were decisive ones. I learned little, because I left my mother at an early age, roamed at large, and soon became accustomed to independence; premature independence is inimical to the systematic acquisition of knowledge. But I saw and heard many things. I talked to dogs of all sorts and degrees, and understood reasonably well what I was told; integrating single observations into the whole, that stood in to some extent for erudition, and besides, independence, though it may be a disadvantage where the acquisition of knowledge is concerned, yet for research it is a great advantage. It was all the more necessary in my case because I was unable to follow the proper scientific method, which would have been to use the work of predecessors and to seek out my scientific contemporaries. Instead, I was utterly self-reliant, I began at the very beginning, and with the awareness—so enchanting to the young, so profoundly dispiriting for the elderly—that whatever chance point I happened to reach would also define my whole endeavor. But was I really so alone with my investigations, all this time? Yes and no. It is impossible to think that the odd dog hasn't found himself—doesn't find himself today—in my situation. Things can't be that desperate for me. I am not a hair's breadth outside the doggish norm. Every dog has, as I do, the urge to question. And I, like all dogs, have the compulsion to be silent. All have the urge to ask questions. Could my questions otherwise have had the least effect, which I was fortunate enough to behold with delight, albeit greatly overstated delight? And the fact that I also have a compulsion to silence, that needs no particular support. Fundamentally, then, I am not so different from any other dog, and that is why basically everyone will recognize me and I them, despite the differences of opinion and taste that may exist between us. Only the proportion of the constituent elements varies; to me personally. the difference is substantial, but in terms of the species as a whole it is negligible. How should the mixture of elements, either now or in the past, not have given rise to the likes of myself or even (if one wants to call the result unfortunate in my case), something still more unfortunate? Why, that would fly in the face of all experience. We dogs are busy in the most varied professions and callings, such professions as one would hardly credit, if it wasn't that one had the most reliable information about them.

I like to think at this point about air dogs. The first time I heard of one such, I laughed and refused to be persuaded of their existence. What?! A minuscule dog, not much bigger than my head, even when fully mature, and this dog, utterly feeble of course—by appearances an artificial, immature, excessively coiffed thing, quite incapable of an honest to goodness leap—a dog like this was said to move largely through the air, and without any visible effort either, but to do so in a state of rest. No, to seek to convince me of such a thing was to take advantage of the earnest credulousness of a young dog, or so I thought. But then I heard tell, from a separate source, of a second air dog. Was this some sort of conspiracy to make fun of me? This was when I encountered the musician dogs, and from that time forth, I thought everything was possible. I allowed no prejudice to set limits to my imagination, I pursued the most outrageous rumors, investigating them to the best of my ability; the most senseless things in this farraginous thing we call life seemed to be more plausible than any amount of sense, and in terms of my research, especially useful. These air dogs were one example. I learned a lot about them, to this day I haven't actually seen one, but I became convinced of their existence long ago, and they occupy an important place in my overall scheme of things. As is usually the case, so here it is not the art that gives me pause. It's wonderful—who could deny it—that these dogs are able to float through the air: in my astonishment I am one with the rest of dogdom. But much more wonderful to me is the overall feeling of farrago, the silent unreasonableness of these beings. In general there is no cause given for it—they float through the air, and that's our lot; life goes on, here and there they talk of art and artists, and that's it. But why, oh kindly dogdom, why do these particular dogs float? What point is there in their calling? Why no word of explanation from the creatures themselves? Why do they float up there, letting their legs, which are our pride and joy, atrophy from being parted from the nourishing mother earth, not sowing, merely reaping, apparently even being nourished particularly well by providential dogdom.

I flatter myself that by my questions I may have stirred up these things. One begins to seek causes, to stammer together a kind of etiology—yes, one begins, and of course will never get beyond the beginning. But it's something—a beginning. The truth may not appear—one won't get that far—but at least something of the deeply rooted nature of the lie. All the nonsensical aspects of life, most especially the most nonsensical ones, allow themselves to be justified. Not completely—that's the fiendish nature of what one is up against—but enough to guard against difficult questions. I'll take the air dogs by way of example again. They are not arrogant, as one might at first have supposed; they are if anything perhaps especially needy of their fellow dogs. If you try and put yourself in their position, you will understand. Even if they can't do so openly—that would violate the rule of silence—they are obliged in one way or another to seek absolution for their way of life, or at least to distract from it, obscure it, which they do, so I am told, by their almost unbearable garrulousness. They are forever holding forth, whether about their philosophy, to which, since they have almost completely abandoned physical exertion, they are able to devote themselves, or about the observations they are able to make from their comparative altitude. And even though they don't shine in terms of their intellect, which is only too understandable given the frivolous nature of their lives, and their philosophy is as worthless as their observations so that they become almost useless to science, which fortunately doesn't depend on such miserable auxiliary sources, even so, when you ask what air dogs are for, the answer you keep hearing is that they contribute an awful lot to science. "True," you reply, "only it's a lot that is worthless and maddening." The next answer is a shrug of the shoulders, a change of subject, a show of irritation or laughter, and in a while, the next time you ask, it is only to be told again that they contribute to science, and finally, should the question be put to you, you don't think about it too much and you make the very same reply. And maybe it's a good thing not to be too obdurate and to give in, maybe not conceding those air dogs already extant have some purpose in their lives, which would be impossible, but at least to tolerate them. You can't ask for more than that, and then of course you do. You ask for tolerance to be extended to more and more air dogs as they multiply. You don't exactly know where they come from. Do they procreate by the conventional method? Do they have the strength? After all there's not much more to them than a beautiful pelt, so what there is going to actually procreate? And if the improbable should happen, when would it take place? They are only ever seen in splendid isolation and if they condescend to run around at all, it's only for a little while, a few sashaying strides and always lost—it is claimed—in solitary thought, from which, even if they tried, they cannot break free. At least so they tell us. If these creatures don't manage to procreate, is it conceivable that dogs would come forward who freely renounce life on terra firma, in order to become air dogs, and in exchange for a modicum of comfort and a certain technical prestige, choose that arid, pillowed life?

I say no. I think neither procreation nor voluntary renunciation is conceivable. But the facts prove to us that there are always new air dogs around; from this we are driven to conclude that even if the hindrances are insuperable in our understanding, a breed of dogs once in existence and however peculiar will not be rendered extinct—or at least not easily, not without some aspect in each breed that will stick up for itself long and hard. And then, am I not compelled to think, if this holds true for such an eccentric, meaningless, visually freakish, unviable breed as the air dog, will it not equally hold true for my own? And I am externally not at all out of the run of dogs that is very often met with, at least in these parts, in no way either conspicuous or contemptible; certainly in my youth and still to some degree into manhood, as long as I didn't neglect myself and took a modicum of exercise, I was a moderately attractive specimen, my front aspect especially came in for praise, my trim legs, the graceful carriage of my head, but also my gray-white-yellow fur, curling at the ends was much admired; but none of it stood out, the only remarkable thing about me is my nature, but even that, as I never tire of pointing out, is squarely rooted in the general canine character. Now, if the air dog is not left celibate, and here and there in greater dogdom a willing individual is found, and they can produce heirs even *ex nihilo*, then why may I not be certain that I have not been abandoned? Of course my fellow dogs must have a particular destiny, and their existence will never visibly help me, not least because I will never acknowledge them. We are those who are oppressed by silence, who break it merely in order to breathe; the others seem to feel at ease in it, though that is only in appearance, as with the musical dogs, who were in harmony and apparent tranquility, while in reality they were tremendously agitated. But the outward appearance is strong—one may seek to outwit it, but it mocks all our attempts.

So how do my fellow dogs help one another? What kind of attempts do they make to live in spite of everything? What do they look like? There are probably different answers. I tried with my attempts at questioning, while I was young. It might be an idea to stick to those who are given to asking questions themselves, and then I would have some company. For a time I tried that too, in spite of myself, because the ones that most bother me are the ones from whom I want answers; the ones who keep butting in with questions I usually can't answer are merely repulsive to me. Anyway, who doesn't like to ask questions while he's still young? How am I to find the right ones among the many, many questioners? One question sounds much like another, it's a matter of the intention behind it, which is often concealed even from the questioner. Anyway, questioning is an idiosyncrasy among dogs; they ask their questions all at once, as though to conceal the traces of the real questioner. No, I won't find a confederate among the questioners, the young ones, any more than I do among the silent ones and the old ones, to whom I now belong. What's the point of questions anyway, I've failed with them; probably my fellow dogs are far cleverer than I am, and apply different and excellent methods of their own for coping with this life, methods, admittedly, that may be useful to them in appeasing or disguising who they are, may calm or lull or disguise what they are, but in general they will be just as ineffectual as mine because, look about me as I may, I see little sign of success in any quarter. I fear I will recognize a confederate by anything but success.

So where are they then? Yes, that's what lies at the heart of my complaint. Where are they? Everywhere and nowhere. It may be my neighbor, three steps away—we often call out to one another, he comes and sees me from time to time—I never visit him. So is he my twin soul? I don't know, I see nothing in him that I recognize, but it's possible. Possible, but hardly likely; if he's somewhere out of sight, in play and using all my imagination, I can indeed discern various suspiciously familiar qualities in him, but when I see him standing in front of me, I have to laugh at my fantasy. An old dog, a little shorter than I am (and I am barely average height), brown, shorthaired, with a tired, drooping head, shuffling gait, and trailing his left hind leg, the consequence of some illness. I've not been on such close terms with anyone for a long time; I'm glad I can manage to tolerate him, and when he goes home I call out the friendliest things after him, not out of affection, but out of self-contempt, because as I watch him turn and go, I find him perfectly repulsive, the way he slinks off with that dragging foot of his and his hindquarters so dismally low to the ground. Sometimes I have the feeling I'm humiliating myself when I think of him as an associate at all. In our conversations he certainly doesn't indicate any sort of association: he is clever, and by our standards here, fairly cultured, and I'm sure there's much I could learn from him, but is it really cleverness and culture I'm looking for? We mostly talk about parochial things and I am regularly astonished—sensitized as I am in this respect by my solitariness—how much mind is required even for an ordinary dog, even in normal, not unduly adverse circumstances, to preserve himself from the standard perils of life. Science gives us rules, but understanding them only from a distance and in rough outline is not easy, and if one has understood them, then the difficult part begins, which is how they apply to local conditions. Hardly anyone can help you with that, almost every hour poses new problems, and every new patch of ground has special difficulties; no one can claim to be well-set for the long run, or that his life takes care of itself, not even I, whose requirements seem to dwindle from one day to the next. And all this effort—to what end? Only to bury yourself so deeply in silence that no one will ever be able to pull you out of it.

We like to celebrate the progress of dogdom; though probably what we mean is the progress of science. Indeed, science makes great strides, it is unstoppable; it even seems to accelerate, move ever more quickly, but what is worth celebrating about that? It's as if someone were to make a great fuss of becoming older with the passing years and approaching death ever more rapidly. I call that a natural process, and not even an attractive one at that, and I find nothing worth celebrating in it. All I see is decline, by which I don't mean that previous generations were superior—no, they were just younger, their memory was not so burdened as ours today, it was easier to get them to speak, and even if no one succeeded in doing it, the sense of possibility was greater, and it is this greater potential that so rouses us as we listen to those old, really rather unsophisticated stories. Every now and again we hear a promising word, and it's almost enough to get us to leap up, if it wasn't that we felt the burden of the centuries weighing us down. No, whatever I have against my own time, previous generations were no better, and in some respects they were much feebler and much worse. Miracles weren't performed in the streets then to be apprehended by all and sundry, but the dogs were somehow—I can think of no other way of saying this—not as doggish as they are today, dogdom was more loosely associated, the true word could have played a role, to change or revise the structure, at anyone's will, even turning it into its opposite, and the word at least felt close at hand, it was on the tip of the tongue, anyone could learn it. Today, where has it got to, today one could reach into the bowels of language and not find it! Our generation may be lost, but it is more innocent than its predecessors. I can understand our hesitation; in fact it's no longer just hesitation, it's the forgetting of a dream dreamed and forgotten for the first time a thousand nights ago. Who would hold it against us that we have forgotten it for the thousandth time?

But I can understand the hesitation of our forefathers too. We probably wouldn't have behaved any differently: I almost feel like saying, good for us, that it wasn't us who had to shoulder the guilt; rather that, in a world already darkened by others, we had to hasten toward death in an almost guilt-free silence. When our forefathers lost their way, they probably wouldn't have thought of an unending wilderness; they could probably still see the crossroads and it would have been easy enough to return there at any time, so only because they wanted to enjoy their dogs' lives a little longer—it wasn't really a dog's life, and if it already struck them as intoxicatingly lovely, imagine what it would be like later, at least a little later—they wandered on. They didn't know what we can now sense from our contemplation of history, that the soul changes faster than life does, and that when their dog's life began to please them, they must already have had ancient souls, and they weren't as close to the starting point as maybe they thought, or as their eye, delighting in all those doggish joys, tried to convince them was the case. Who today can still speak of youth in any meaningful way? They were the true young dogs, but unfortunately their only ambition was to become old dogs, something they couldn't fail at, as every subsequent generation proves, and ours, the latest, proves best of all.

All these were things that of course I didn't speak of to my neighbor, but I often think of them when sitting with him, that typical old dog, or bury my muzzle in his fur, which already has something of the smell of a carcass. It would be pointless to talk about those things, with him or anyone else. I know what course the conversation would follow. He would offer a few little objections here and there, but in the end he would agree with me—agreement is our best defense—and the issue would be laid to rest. Why even bother digging it up in the first place? And yet, in spite of everything, there is perhaps a deeper accord with my neighbor that goes beyond mere words. I won't stop insisting on it, even though I have no evidence for it, and am perhaps subject simply to a very basic delusion, because he's the only party I've been in communication with for a long time, and so I am obliged to stick to him. "Are you perhaps my comrade after all? In your own way? And you're ashamed because it's all gone wrong? See, I feel exactly the same way. When I'm alone, I cry about it; come, if there are two of us, it'll be sweeter." That's what I think sometimes and fix his eye. He doesn't lower his glance, but there's nothing to be heard from him either; he looks at me expressionlessly, and wonders why I have allowed a break in our conversation, and don't say anything. But perhaps that look is his way of asking, and I disappoint him, just as he disappoints me. In my youth, if no other questions had seemed more important to me and I had had enough of myself, then I might have asked him out loud, might have got his quiet agreement in response, less than today, when he's silent. But isn't everyone silent? What keeps me from believing that they're all my comrades, that I didn't just find the occasional fellow researcher, sunk and forgotten along with his insignificant results, inaccessible beyond the darkness of the times, or the hustle of the present; but instead that I have had comrades in everyone always, all of them, in keeping with their nature, trying hard, all without success, all taciturn or gabby, as is bound to be the case, with these hopeless investigations. But then I would never have had to remain aloof, I could have stayed with the others, wouldn't have had to barge my way out like an ill-bred child through lines of grown-ups, all of whom wanted to get on as much as I did, and whose experience it is that confounds me, namely that no one will get on, and that all attempts to push out are foolish.

Such thoughts are undoubtedly influenced by my neighbor; he confuses me, he makes me melancholy; and yet he's happy enough by himself, at least when I hear him on his patch, calling out and singing in that irritating way of his. It would be good to dispense with this last element of society, not to pursue vague dreams of the sort that any dealings with dogs are bound to produce, no matter how tough you think you've become, and to use the little bit of time remaining to me exclusively for my investigations. The next time he comes calling, I will hide away and pretend to be asleep, and I will do that until he finally gives up altogether.

Also a measure of disorganization has crept into my research. I am falling behind, I am getting tired, I just trot along mechanically, where once I would leap ahead enraptured. I'm thinking back to the time when I first began to investigate the question "Where does the earth take our nourishment from?" Then, admittedly, I lived amongst the crowd, I forced my way in where they were at their densest, I wanted everyone to be a witness to my work, their observations were even more important to me than my work, since I was still in expectation of some sort of general effect. That of course gave me huge encouragement, which as a solitary dog I no longer get. At that time, though, I was so strong that I did something unheard of, something that flies in the face of all our principles, and that any eyewitness from the time will recall as extraordinary. I found in one aspect of the science, which generally favors extreme specialization, a curious simplification. It teaches us that it is principally the earth that produces our food, and, having stated that, goes on to list the methods by which the various foods can be produced in their best condition and their greatest abundance. Now it's true of course, food does come from the ground, there is no doubting that, but it's really not so simple as in that bald statement, to the extent that it excludes all further research. Take the type of primitive incident that occurs every day. If we were wholly idle (as I in fact already almost am) and after perfunctorily tending the soil we rolled ourselves up and waited for what was coming, then we would indeed find our food on the ground—assuming, that is, that there was any food forthcoming at all. But this is hardly the rule. Whoever has managed to retain a modicum of openmindedness vis-à-vis the science—and there are not many, as the circles that science likes to trace are ever expanding—will easily see, even in the absence of specific observations, that the greater part of the nourishment on the ground will have come from above; sometimes, depending on our dexterity and the degree of our hunger, we even manage to intercept most of it before it touches the ground at all. Now, I'm not saying anything against the science; of course it's the earth that produces this nourishment, whether it summons it up from itself or calls it down from above hardly matters, and the science that has established that working the ground is necessary perhaps doesn't need to get itself involved in any more detail than that; after all, as we like to say: "If you've got your munchies in your mouth, your problems are over for the time being." But it seems to me that

at least in a veiled way, science is partly concerned with these
things, seeing that it does acknowledge there are two principal methods of sourcing food, namely working the soil and
then the subtly complementary activities of speech, dance,
and song. While this may not be a complete dichotomy, it
does seem to bear out my distinction. In my opinion, tilling
the ground works to secure both types of nourishment and is
always indispensable; speech, dance, and song are less concerned with ground provisioning in the strict sense, and more
with the drawing down of sustenance from above. In adopting this view, I am supported by tradition. Here the populace
corrects science without apparently knowing it, and without
science daring to oppose it. If, as science likes to claim, those
ceremonies are exclusively concerned with serving the soil,
say by giving it strength, then to be logical they would have
to be performed on the ground, and everything would have
to be whispered, chanted, and danced in the direction of the
ground. So far as I know, that's what science would have us do
anyway. But here's the thing: the popular ceremonies are directed at the air. It's not a violation of science, science doesn't
seek to stamp it out, it leaves the ploughman his discretion;
in its teachings it is focused entirely on the soil, and if the
ploughman performs these teachings on the ground, then it
is satisfied, but its thinking, to my mind, should really be
more sophisticated. And I, who was never deeply inducted
into science, cannot for the life of me imagine how learned
men can tolerate our people, passionate as they are, calling
out the magic words into the air, wailing our old folk lamentations at the air, and performing leaping dances as if, quite
forgetting the ground, they wanted to hang in the air forever.
My starting point was to stress these contradictions. Each
time that, according to the principles of science, harvest time

drew near, I confined my attentions to the soil; I scraped it in my dancing, I twisted my head to be as close to it as I could; later I dug a furrow for my muzzle and sang and declaimed in such a way that only the ground might hear it and no one else above me or beside me.

The results of my research were inconclusive: sometimes I was given no food and was on the point of jubilation about my discovery, but then the food presented itself, as though initially perplexed by the eccentricity of my original performance. And now, seeing its advantages, and happy to dispense with my shouts and leaps, often the food came more abundantly than before, though there were other times when none was forthcoming at all. With an industry unknown previously in young dogs, I kept exact records of all my experiments, and from time to time thought I had found a sign that would take me further, but then it was lost in the sand. Impossible to deny, too, that my lack of scientific background was a handicap. How could I prove for instance that the unforthcomingness of food was not brought on by some fault with my experiment—unscientific tilling of the ground, for instance—and if that was the case, then all my results were void. There was a perfectly precise experiment I could have conducted, that is, if I had succeeded without preparing the ground at all and then purely through a vertically directed ceremony in getting the lowering of the food, while by groundwork alone the food had failed to appear. I attempted something of the kind, but without real conviction and not under laboratory conditions, because I remain unshakeably convinced that a certain measure of preparing the ground is essential; and even if those heretics who don't believe it were right, it still couldn't be proved, since the sprinkling of the ground takes place under pressure and up to a point is not wholly voluntary. I had more success with a different, rather unusual experiment that attracted a certain amount of attention. In a variant of the usual interception of food in midair, I decided not to allow the food to fall to the ground, but not to intercept it either. To that end, I would perform a little leap in the air that was calculatedly inept; usually what happened was that it fell dully to the ground, and I would hurl myself upon it in a fury, not just of hunger but of disappointment. But in a few cases, something else happened, something actually rather miraculous: the food would not drop, but would follow me in the air—the food would follow the hungry individual. This didn't take place in any sustained way—just for brief spells—and then it would fall after all, or disappear altogether or—this was the usual outcome—my greed would bring a premature end to the experiment and I wolfed down whatever it was.

Still, I was happy at the time, there was a buzz around me, others were unsettled by me and began to take an interest, I found my acquaintances more open to my questions, in their eyes I saw the appeal for help; and even if it was nothing more than the reflection of my own look, I wanted nothing more, I was content. Until I learned—and others learned with me—that this experiment had been written up in science long ago, in a far grander version than mine, though it hadn't been performed for a long time because of the degree of self-control it calls for, and also on account of its alleged scientific insignificance. It proved, so they said, only what was already known, namely that the ground does not collect nourishment in a direct vertical line, but at an angle, or even in a spiral.

So there I was, but I wasn't at all discouraged, I was much too young for that; on the contrary, I felt emboldened to attempt what was perhaps the greatest achievement of my life.

I didn't believe that my experiment was ultimately discredited, but this wasn't a question of belief, but of proof, and I wanted to acquire it, and thus place my originally somewhat eccentric experiment under the harsh light and focus of science. I wanted to prove that when I shrank back from the nourishment, it wasn't the ground that drew it down at an angle, but myself drawing it on to me. I wasn't able to expand the experiment; to see the munchies in front of me and to go on experimenting scientifically is more than any dog can stand in the long run. But I purposed something else. I wanted to go on a fast for as long as I could bear it, while avoiding all sight of food and all temptation. If I withdrew in such a fashion, remained lying there with eyes closed day and night, attempted neither the picking up nor the intercepting of food, and as I didn't dare claim but privately hoped, without any of the usual measures save the inevitable uncontrolled irrigation of the soil and quiet recital of speech and song (I would renounce the function of dance so as not to weaken myself), the food would descend of its own accord and, without bothering with the ground, would crave entry by knocking against my teeth—if this were to happen, then I wouldn't have overturned the science, because science is sufficiently elastic for exceptions and isolated cases, but what would the people say, who happily possess less in the way of elasticity? After all, this wouldn't be an exception of the sort that is handed down in stories—someone, say, with a physical malady or mental impairment refusing to work for their food, to look for it, or to consume it, upon which dogdom would assemble and recite formulas of invocation and secure a movement of the food from its usual path directly into the mouth of the afflicted party. I was in the pink, my appetite was so healthy that for days I could think of nothing else; I submitted, believe it or not, voluntarily to fasting, I was myself fully responsible for the downward course of the nourishment, I needed no help from dogdom, and even explicitly forbade it.

I sought out an appropriate place in a remote shrubbery where I would hear no talk of food, no smacking of lips or cracking of bones, filled my belly one last time, and then lay down. It was my idea to spend all the time if possible with my eyes closed; so long as no food came, it should be night as far as I was concerned, and it would go on for days and weeks. The great difficulty was that I should not sleep either, or at least as little as possible, because I had not only to be summoning down the food to me, but also I had to be on guard lest I sleep through its coming; on the other hand, of course sleep was most welcome, because I would be able to go on fasting for much longer asleep than awake. With these thoughts, I decided to divide my time very carefully and sleep a lot, but only in very short spells. I managed this by propping my head on a thin branch that would quickly bend and thereby wake me. So there I lay, asleep or awake, dreaming or silently singing to myself. To begin with, time passed wholly uneventfully, perhaps it had not been observed, wherever food was distributed, that I was absent, opposing the usual run of things, and so all was quiet. I was a little disturbed in my endeavor by the fear that the dogs would miss me, find me and undertake some action against me. A second fear was lest, in response to a mere sprinkling, the ground, even though by the light of science it was infertile ground, would provide some so-called inadvertent nourishment, and its smile could beguile me. But for the moment nothing like that happened, and I was able to go on starving myself. My fears aside, I was quite calm to begin with, in a way I can't remember having been before. Even though I was working against science, I felt a great contentment—almost the proverbial calm of the scientific worker. In my dreams I obtained science's indulgence; I felt assured that it also had room for my inquiries, it sounded very soothing in my ears that, however successful my research ended up being (and especially then), I would not be lost to the ordinary life of dogs; science cast a kindly eye on me, it promised it would get to work on the interpretation of my findings, and that promise to me was fulfillment itself; I would, even as I felt expelled in my innermost being, and charged the walls of my tribe like a wild thing, I would be received with honors, the longed-for warmth of assembled dogsbodies would flow around me, I would be carried swaying, shoulder high by my people. Hunger can have a powerful effect on those unaccustomed to it. My achievement seemed to me such that out of self-pity I began to cry in my shrubbery, which didn't quite make sense since, if I was expecting the reward I'd earned, why cry? Out of sheer contentment. I never liked to cry. Whenever I felt satisfaction, which was rarely enough, I cried. At least it was soon over. The pretty pictures faded gradually as my hunger grew, and it didn't take long until fantasies and emotion had been purged and I was completely alone with the burning sensation in my intestines. "That's what hunger feels like," I said to myself endlessly, as though to persuade myself that hunger and I were still two separate beings, and I could shake it off like a tedious lover, but in reality we were a very painful entity, and when I said to myself, "That's what hunger feels like," then it was really hunger that was speaking and thus making fun of me. An awful, awful time! I still shudder to remember it, not just on account of the suffering I endured, but because I didn't see it through to the end; because I will have to go through this hunger again if I am to achieve anything; because starvation is to me still the ultimate and most powerful tool in my investigations. The way leads through starvation; the highest is only attainable through the most extreme privation, and for us this privation is voluntary fasting.

So when I think back to those times—and I love to brood over them—I think too about the times that loom ahead. It seems you have to almost let your life pass by before you recover from such an experiment; my entire manhood separates me from that period of starvation, and I still haven't recovered. When next I embark on a period of starvation, I may have more resolve, as a result of my years and my superior understanding of the need for such an experiment, but my forces are still depleted from last time, I can feel myself sapped already by the prospect of the familiar terrors. My weaker appetite won't help me; at most it will devalue my experiment and probably force me to starve for longer than I would have had to then. I think I am clear about these and other assumptions, it's not that the long time in between has been without trial runs—often enough I have clamped my teeth round hunger, but I wasn't strong enough for the ultimate test—and the uninhibited get-up-and-go of youth is of course gone now. It faded while I was fasting that first time.

Some considerations tormented me. I saw the menacing spectres of our forefathers. Though I don't say so openly, I blame them for everything: they brought us the dog's life, and I could easily reply to their threats with counterthreats of my own; but I bow to their knowledge, it came from sources that are no longer known to us, which is why, however much I am opposed to them, I would never disregard their laws, but just beetle toward the little chinks in them for which I have a keen perception. Where hunger is concerned,

I appeal to a famous conversation in the course of which one of our sages pronounced the intention of outlawing starvation, from which another tried to dissuade him with the question: "Who would ever think of starving themselves?" and the former allowed himself to be persuaded and dropped the idea of the ban. Now the question comes around again: "Isn't starving yourself actually forbidden?" The great majority of commentators deny it, they see fasting as lawful, they take the part of the second wise man and are therefore not afraid of bad consequences flowing from their misleading comment. I had taken care to establish the facts before embarking on my program. But now that I was writhing with hunger, and in my mental confusion kept having recourse to my hind legs, desperately licking, gnawing, sucking them all the way up to my bottom, the general interpretation of that conversation struck me as completely false. I cursed the commentators' science, I cursed myself for having allowed myself to be misled by them; the conversation contained, as any child would see—given that it was a starving child— more than one ban on fasting; the first wise man wanted to forbid it, and whatever one wise man wants to do is already done, so hunger was already outlawed; and the second wise man not only agreed with him but even took hunger to be impossible, in effect balancing a second embargo on top of the first, this embargo deriving from the canine character itself; the first one understood this and therefore withheld the explicit embargo, that is, after discussion, he urged dogs to be prudent and simply to forswear starvation. In effect, it was a triple ban instead of the usual single one, and I had violated it.

Now I could at least have heeded it belatedly and stopped starving myself, but running right through the pain was a

kind of temptation, and I followed its trail, as if lusting after an unknown scent. I couldn't stop, perhaps I was already
too weak to get up and return to inhabited areas. I tossed
and turned on my forest floor, sleeping was beyond me, I
heard sounds everywhere; the world that had been asleep
through my previous life seemed to have been brought to
life by my hunger, I had the notion that I would never eat
again, because then I would have to silence the whole world,
and that was beyond me; admittedly the very loudest noise
of all was in my stomach; I often pressed my ear against it
and must have looked appalled because I could hardly believe what I was hearing. And as things were really getting
bad, my senses became disorientated as well, and I thought
of crazy ways of saving myself: I started smelling foods, exquisite things I hadn't eaten for ages, the joys of my infancy,
yes, I could smell the teats of my mother. I forgot my resolve to resist smells, or rather I didn't; with determination,
as though it were a resolution I'd set myself, I dragged myself around every which way, never more than one or two
paces, and sniffed, as though I were seeking out foods so as
to guard myself against them. The fact that I didn't find any
didn't disappoint me, the food must be there, only it was always a few paces too far away for me, and my legs buckled
before I could reach it. Simultaneously I knew that there
was nothing there at all, that I was just carrying out these
little movements for fear of the moment I would irrevocably
break down somewhere and would never be able to leave.
My last hopes disappeared, the last temptations: I would die
miserably here, what was the point of my investigations,
childish experiments from a childishly happy time; what
was serious was here and now, here was where investigation
could have proved its worth, but where was it? Here was a

dog snapping at nothing, hurriedly and convulsively irrigating the soil over and over, though his memory was incapable of summoning a single line from the whole array of magical sayings, not even the one with which newborns take shelter under their mother.

I felt as though I wasn't just separated by a few yards from my brothers, but was infinitely far from all of them, and as though it wasn't hunger that was killing me so much as my sense of abandonment. It was perfectly clear that no one was bothering about me, no one under the ground, no one over the ground, no one in the heights; I was dying from indifference, the indifference was saying: he is dying, and so it would be. And didn't I agree? Wasn't I saying the same thing? Had I not in fact wanted this abandonment? Yes, you dogs, but not to end here like this, to reach across to the truth from out of this world of lies, where there is no one from whom you can learn the truth, not even me, a born citizen liar. Perhaps the truth wasn't all that far off, but it was too far for me, who was failing and would die. Perhaps it wasn't too far, and then I wasn't as abandoned as I thought either—not by the others, only by myself, failing and dying here.

But the truth is you don't die as quickly as an anxious dog believes. I merely lost consciousness, and when I came round and opened my eyes, there was an unfamiliar dog standing in front of me. I had no feeling of hunger, I felt very strong, in my joints there was a quivering, even though I made no attempt to test it by getting up. I didn't seem to see any more than I did at other times, and yet a fine but hardly outstanding dog was standing in front of me. I saw that— nothing else—and yet I thought I saw more of him than I would ordinarily. There was blood underneath me—my first thought was that it was food, but I noticed soon enough that it was blood that I had vomited. I turned away from it, and toward the strange dog. He was lean, long-legged, tan, here and there with flecks of white, and he had a fine, strong, questing look. "What are you doing here?" he said. "You must leave." "I can't leave now," I said, without further explanation, because how could I have told him everything, and anyway he seemed to be in a hurry. "Please, leave," he said, restlessly picking up his feet in turn. "Let me be," I said. "Go away and forget about me; just like the others have forgotten about me." "Please, for your own sake," he said. "You can ask me for anyone's sake you want," I said, "the fact is I can't leave, even if I wanted to." "That's not the issue," he said, smiling. "You can go. It's because you seem to be weak that I'm begging you to leave in your own time. If you hesitate, you'll only have to run later on." "Let that be my concern," I said. "It's mine too," he said, grieved by my stubbornness, and it was obvious he would have preferred me to stay for the moment, and use the opportunity to approach me in love. At any other time, I would have submitted to such a handsome beast gladly, but just then, I don't know why, I felt aghast at the idea, "Go away," I screamed, all the more loudly as I had no other way of defending myself. "All right, I am going," he said, slowly stepping back. "You're strange. Don't you like me then?" "I will like you once you leave me alone," I said, but I wasn't as sure of myself as I wanted to sound. There was something about him that I could hear or see with my senses sharpened by hunger; it was just beginning, it was growing, it was coming nearer, and already I knew: this dog has the power to drive you away even if you can't yet imagine how you will ever get to your feet. And I looked at him, shaking his head gently at my coarse reply, with ever greater desire. "Who are you?" I asked. "I'm a hunter," he said. "And why don't you want to leave me here?" "You're in the way," he said. "I can't hunt with you here." "Try," I said, "perhaps you will be able to." "No," he said, "I'm sorry, but you need to go." "Forget about hunting for the day!" I asked him. "No," he said, "I've got to." "I've got to leave, and you've got to hunt," I said. "Lots of gots there. Do you understand why?" "No," he said, "but there's nothing to understand either, these are all perfectly reasonable, natural things." "Not at all," I said, "you're sorry to have to chase me away, and still you do it." "That's true," he said. "That's true," I mimicked crossly, "what kind of answer is that? What would be easier for you: not to hunt or not to drive me away?" "Not to hunt," he said without any hesitation. "Well then," I said, "you're contradicting yourself." "Where's the contradiction?" he asked. "You dear little dog, don't you understand that I have to? Don't you understand perfectly natural things?" I didn't say anything because I noticed—and a kind of new life surged through me, a life that was sparked by a sense of dread— from certain elusive details that maybe no one but me could have noticed, that this dog was opening his chest to make ready to sing. "You're about to sing," I said. "Yes," he said seriously, "I'm going to sing—soon, but not yet." "You're already beginning," I said. "No," he said, "not yet. But prepare yourself." "Deny it all you want, I can hear it," I said, trembling. He made no reply. And I thought I could tell what no dog before me had ever noticed—at least in our traditions there are no hints of it—and in endless panic and shame I hurriedly lowered my face to the puddle of blood in front of me. I thought I could tell that the dog was already singing without knowing it, yes, and more, that the melody, separate from him, was floating through the air following its own laws, through him and past him, as though it wasn't anything to do with him, and was only aiming for me. Today of course I will deny all such perceptions and merely ascribe them to my over-stimulated condition, but even if it was an illusion, it does have something magnificent about it, as the only apparent reality I managed to salvage from that period of starvation, and shows how far we can travel if we are completely beside ourselves, as I was then.

And I really was beside myself then. Under normal circumstances, I would have been seriously ill and unable to move, but I couldn't withstand the melody the dog would soon take up as his. It grew ever stronger; its welling seemed to know no bounds, already it was almost shattering my hearing. But the worst thing was that it seemed to exist only on my account, the voice before whose loftiness the forest hushed, was just for me; and who was I to dare to stay here sprawled out in front of it in blood and filth. Shaking, I got to my feet and looked down the length of my body; "that body can't walk," I managed to think to myself, but already chased by the melody, I was flying along in exquisite bounds. I said nothing of this to my friends; right after my arrival I would probably have blabbed, but I was too weak, and later on it simply struck me that such things could not be communicated. Hints that I couldn't force myself to suppress were lost without trace in our conversations. Physically, I was restored in a matter of hours, though my spirit still bears the scars today.

I expanded the scope of my investigations to include canine music. Science had not been idle in this field either; the study of music, if I am correctly informed, is perhaps even more extensive than that of food and certainly more solidly based. This can be accounted for because the terrain can be worked over more dispassionately; it tends to be a matter of observation and systematization, whereas in that other field there are practical consequences to be weighed up as well. It is musical science, accordingly, that is more respected than nutritional science, though the first can never be as deeply rooted in our people. Also my attitude toward musical science was more agnostic than any other—until I heard the voice in the forest. My experience with the canine musicians had already pointed me the way, but I was still too young at the time, nor is it easy to get to grips with that science; it is reckoned to be particularly arcane, and difficult of access. Also, while the music had been the most arresting aspect of those dogs, what seemed more important to me then was the discretion of their being, their terrible music was like nothing I had ever known, making it easier for me to set it aside, whereas their nature was what I encountered in dogs everywhere. To penetrate the true nature of dogs, the study of nutrition seemed to promise the most direct route. Perhaps I was wrong to think so. The contiguity of the two sciences had already caught my attention. It's the lesson of the song that brings down nourishment. Again, it is much to my regret that I never made a serious study of musical science; I can't even count myself among those semieducated individuals who attract the most contempt from experts. I need to keep this in mind always. Given an elementary test by an expert, I would fare badly indeed—and unfortunately I have proof of this. This has its roots, in addition to biographical circumstances mentioned already, in my lack of scientific ability, poor capacity for abstract thought, worse memory, and above all my inability to keep a scientific goal always before me. I admit all this to myself quite openly, even with a certain relish. Because the deeper ground for my scientific inability seems to me to be an instinct, and not a bad instinct at that. Were I to brag, I could say that it was this instinct that has destroyed my abilities as a scientist, because wouldn't it be odd after all, if I—who in the ordinary things of daily living, which are certainly not the simplest, demonstrate a tolerable comprehension, if not of science, then at least of scientists, as witness my results—if I should have been unable from the very beginning to raise my paw to the lowest rung of science. This was the instinct that—perhaps out of regard for science, but a different sort of science from that practiced today, an ultimate science—has led me to esteem freedom more highly than anything else. Freedom! Freedom as it is on offer to us today is a wretched weed. But it's freedom of a kind, something to possess.

The Married Couple

The overall state of the business is so poor that when my timetable permits, I sometimes pick up my old sample case and call on clients in person. Among others, I had long meant to visit K., with whom I used to be in regular contact, though this had practically come to an end over the course of the past year, for reasons unknown to me. Disruptions like this actually require no particular cause; in today's difficult circumstances, a trifle, a mood is enough, and another trifle, a mere word, is enough to restore things to what they had been. Going to K.'s is a little awkward; he is an old man, rather frail of late, and even if he still has a firm grip on the business, he rarely goes into the office anymore; if you want to talk to him, you have to visit him at home, and that sort of contact is most apt to be postponed.

But last night, a little after six, I did finally go; it wasn't exactly a conventional visiting time, but then it wasn't a social call so much as a business matter. I was in luck: K. was at home; he had just, as I was told in the hall, returned from a stroll with his wife, and was now in the room of his son, who was unwell and bedridden. I was invited to go up; at first I hesitated, but then my desire to get the thing over with prevailed, and I allowed myself, in hat and coat and sample case, to be conducted through an unlit room into another, dimly lit, where a small group of people were huddled together.

It was probably instinct that caused my first look to fall on the—to me—very familiar figure of a certain business agent, an occasional rival of mine. So he had managed to get the advantage over me, and sneak up ahead. He was sitting comfortably close to the sickbed, almost as if he had been the doctor; he cut a rather powerful figure in his fine, unbuttoned, puffed-up coat. His impertinence is unrivaled; the invalid may well have entertained similar thoughts as he lay there with fever-flushed cheeks, looking up at him from time to time. This son is, by the way, no longer young, he's a man of my own age, with a short beard, a little unkempt from his illness. Old K., a large, broad-shouldered man, though bowed and uncertain and to my astonishment drastically slimmed down on account of his creeping malady, was still standing there in his fur, as though he'd just walked in, murmuring something in the direction of his son. His wife, who was small and fragile-looking, but very animated, at least where he was concerned—she barely noticed the rest of us—was busy trying to take his coat off, which, in view of the difference in height between them, was a difficult undertaking, but finally she succeeded. Perhaps the real difficulty lay in the fact that K. was very impatient, and with fumbling hands kept feeling for the armchair, which, once she had taken off his coat, his wife quickly pushed under him. She herself took the fur, under which she almost disappeared, and carried it away.

Now at last the moment seemed to me to have come—or rather it hadn't come and would probably not come here at all—but if I was going to attempt anything, it would have to be right away because to go by my feeling, the conditions for a clear-the-air business conversation would only get worse; to put down roots, as the other agent apparently intended doing, wasn't my style; and I was determined not to pay any attention to him anyway. So I launched straight into my topic, even though I could see that K. evidently wanted to talk to his son a little. Unfortunately it's my habit, if I have talked myself into a bit of a lather—and that tends to happen quickly, and occurred in this sickroom a little more quickly than usual—to get up and pace about while talking. In one's own office, it's a perfectly viable habit; in someone else's flat it may appear a little uncouth. But I was unable to master myself, especially as I didn't have the customary cigarette. Well, everyone has their habits, and I must say I still prefer mine to those of the agent. What words are there for someone sitting there with his hat on his knee, pushing it slowly to and fro; sometimes suddenly, perfectly unexpectedly, jamming it on his head, then taking it off again right away, as though it had been an accident; but it remains the case that it was on his head for a moment or two; and then he did it again, and again. A performance like that is really beyond the pale. It doesn't bother me, of course; I walk up and down, I'm completely taken up with my own stuff, and I ignore it, but there may be people who find this hat trick utterly discombobulating. When I get the bit between my teeth, not only do I not have eyes for such a disturbance, but I can't see anyone at all; I have a vague sense of what's going on, but until I've finished, or unless I'm actually interrupted, I don't attend to it. So, for example, I noticed that K. had very little attention to give; he was twisting his hands up and down on the armrests of his chair, he didn't look over to me, but peered emptily into the void, and with such an apathetic expression it was as though not a syllable of my speech, not even any sense of my physical presence reached him. His whole (to me) discouraging, possibly morbid behavior I could see perfectly well, but I went on talking, as though I had some prospect through my words, through my advantageous offers—I was alarmed myself about the sweeteners I had offered, sweeteners that no one had asked for—to get back to some kind of equilibrium. It did give me some slight satisfaction when I happened to notice that the agent had stopped playing with his hat and had crossed his arms over his chest; my exposition, which was indeed partly for his benefit, seemed to have put a dampener on his efforts. And in the resulting sense of well-being, I might have gone on speaking for a long time, had not the son, whom I had thus far taken for a minor player here, suddenly half-sat up in bed and, brandishing his fist, brought me to a halt. He clearly wanted to say something himself—to show something—but he lacked the strength. At first I thought it was on account of his fever, but when I involuntarily happened to look at old K. shortly afterward, I understood better.

K. was sitting there with open, glassy, puffy, almost sightless eyes, trembling as he leaned over, as though some adversary had gripped him by the neck or was beating him—his lower lip, yes, his entire jaw with gums exposed hung down helplessly, his entire face was out of kilter; he was still managing to breathe, rather heavily, but then, as though freed, he slumped back against the chair-rest, shut his eyes, the expression of some great exertion crossing his face, and then it was over. Straightaway I leaped to him, touched the cold, lifeless, shudder-inducing hand that dangled there; there was no pulse. So it was all over. Admittedly, he was an old man. May our deaths be no harder than his. But how many things there were to do now! And which one first, in the rush? I looked about me for help; but the son had pulled the blanket over his head and I could hear his steady sobbing; the agent, as cold as a frog, sat tight in his chair, just two steps from K., visibly resolved not to do anything but await developments; so I, I was the only one left to do something, and the hardest thing of all, namely to break it to his wife somehow, in some bearable way—an option that just wasn't available in the world at the moment. Already I could hear the brisk shuffling of her feet from the next room.

She—still in her street clothes, she hadn't had a moment to get changed yet—was bringing a nightshirt that had been warmed through on the stove that she wanted to put on her husband. "He's fallen asleep," she said with a smile and a shake of the head, finding us all so still. And with the unending trustfulness of the innocent, she took the same hand I had just—with some disgust and aversion—held in mine, kissed it in some little marital game, and—the expressions on our three faces, looking on!—K. stirred, yawned loudly, allowed himself to be dressed in the nightshirt, bore with a long-suffering expression the tender reproaches of his wife for having overtired himself in the course of their walk, and countered, to come up with a different explanation for having dropped off, a little remarkably, with something about boredom. Then, to avoid catching a chill on the way to another room, he provisionally slipped into bed with his son; beside the feet of the son, his head was settled on a couple of bolsters hurriedly produced by his wife. After all that had taken place so far, I found nothing unusual in these proceedings. Now he called for the evening paper, took it without regard to his visitors, didn't read it but glanced at a page or column here or there, telling us with astonishing acuity some rather unflattering things about our offers, while continually making dismissive motions with his free hand, and by clacking his tongue suggesting a bad taste in his mouth that our business practices had given him. The agent was unable to bite back a few inappropriate remarks himself, clearly some sort of equilibrium needed to be achieved, but his really wasn't the way to do it. I quickly took my leave, feeling almost grateful to the agent; without his presence I would have lacked the resolve to leave so soon.

In the anteroom I ran into Frau K. At the sight of her wretched form, I told her the first thing that came into my head, namely that she reminded me a little of my mother. And since she stopped still, I added: "Whatever you may say, she was a woman who could perform miracles. All the things we broke that she was able to repair. I lost her when I was still a boy." I had quite deliberately spoken exaggeratedly slowly and distinctly as I assumed the old woman was hard of hearing. But she was probably stone-deaf, since she asked without any pause: "And what about my husband's appearance?" From a few words of goodbye, I could tell she was mistaking me for the agent; I like to think she would have been more cordial otherwise.

Then I went down the steps. Going down was harder than climbing up, which itself hadn't been easy. Oh, the things you do for business, and you still have to go on carrying the load when they fail.

A Commentary

It was very early in the morning, the streets were clean and empty, I was on my way to the station. When I compared my watch with the clock on the bell tower, I saw that it was much later than I had supposed, and I had to hurry; my panic at this discovery made me uncertain of my route, I didn't know this town at all well. Luckily there was a policeman standing there; I ran up to him and, a little out of breath, asked him the way. He smiled and said: "You want me to tell you the way?" "Yes," I said, "I don't think I can find it for myself." "Then give it up," he said, "give it up," and turned away from me with a great flourish, in the manner of someone who wants to be alone with his laughter.

On Parables

Many people complained that the words of the wise were always couched in the form of parables, but were useless in daily life, which is the only sort of life we have. When the wise man says "Cross over," he doesn't mean we should cross over to the other side of the street, which is something one might at least be able to do, if it were worth our while; no, he means some fabulous yonder, some place we don't know, some place that doesn't get any closer description from him either and that therefore can't help us. All these parables are trying to tell us is that the intangible is impossible to grasp, and we knew that anyway. But the things we struggle with every day, those are different.

Thereupon someone said: "Why struggle? If you followed the parables, then you would have become parables yourselves, and thereby free of your daily cares."

Someone else said: "I bet that's a parable as well."

The first person said: "You've won."

The second said: "Yes, but unfortunately only in a parable."

The first man said: "No, in reality; in the parable you've lost."

Homecoming

I have come home; I stride down the passageway and am looking around me. It is my father's old farm. The puddle in the middle of the farmyard. A tangle of useless old gear blocking the steps up to the loft. The cat lurking by the balustrade. A ripped cloth—a plaything—draped once around a pole is flapping in the wind. I have arrived. Who will welcome me? Who is hiding behind the kitchen door? Smoke is coming out the chimney; the water for tea is on the hob. Do you feel in your element, do you feel at home? I don't know, I feel very uncertain. It is my father's house, but the things stand there next to one another coldly, as though each one were busy with its own concerns, which I have partly forgotten, partly never knew. What good can I be to them, what do they care for me, even if I am the son of my father, the old farmer. And I don't dare knock at the kitchen door; I listen out from a distance, standing there, so that I don't get caught listening at the door. And because I am listening from a distance, I manage to hear nothing, only perhaps the sound of a clock striking or perhaps I just think I am hearing it from my childhood. Whatever else is happening in the kitchen is the secret of the people sitting there, which they are keeping from me. What would happen if someone were to open the door now, and ask me a question? Would I not then be like someone wanting to keep his secret to himself?

The Burrow

The burrow is my own design, and I'm happy with the way it's turned out. The only visible trace of it from outside is a big hole, but that in fact goes nowhere; after a couple of feet you encounter bedrock. I don't want to claim it was done that way on purpose, it's just what was left over from one of my many false starts, but in the end I thought it would be a good ruse to leave this one hole unfilled. Many ruses are so obvious that they are self-defeating, that's something I know better than most, and it's certainly a bold stroke to leave the hole to indicate that there may be something worth investigating in the vicinity. But anyone who suspects me of cowardice and my burrow of being a monument to my cowardice misunderstands me. Perhaps a thousand paces from that hole, concealed under a removable flap of moss is the actual entrance to the burrow, it's as secure as anything in this world can be; of course, someone can happen to tread on the moss or push through it, and then my burrow is wide open, and whoever wants to can walk in and destroy it for all time—though it should be pointed out that this requires certain rather rare aptitudes. I understand all that, and even now at its zenith, my life enjoys hardly a single hour of complete quiet; in that place in the dark moss I feel myself mortal, and in my dreams there is often a greedy snout rootling persistently around in it. People will say I should have filled in this actual entrance as well, a thin layer of compact soil at the top, a little looser further down, so that it wouldn't require much effort for me to dig my way out afresh each time. But that isn't possible; prudence actually demands that I have an instantaneous egress, prudence as so often demands the riskier approach; these are all laborious and time-consuming calculations, and the pleasure the shrewd brain takes in itself is sometimes the only reason one goes on calculating. I need instantaneous egress, because is it not conceivable that for all my vigilance I might find myself under attack from some unexpected quarter? There I am, living in peace in the innermost bowels of my burrow, and meanwhile the foe is silently and slowly tunneling toward me. I am not saying his instincts are keener than mine, it's possible that he is as unaware of my existence as I am of his, but there are passionate housebreakers who blindly churn through soil, and given the massive extension of my burrow there is every chance of running into one of my pathways somewhere. Admittedly I have the home advantage here: I have minute knowledge of all the paths and directions. The burglar may very easily become my victim—and a tasty one at that—but I am getting on, there are many who are stronger than I am and the number of my foes is infinite; it could happen that I am running from one of them and wind up in the clutches of another—oh, so many things could happen—at any rate I require the certainty that somewhere there is an easily accessible, fully open exit for me, that requires no further work on my part to reach, so that I never—please God!—find myself digging panic-stricken through loose soil, and feel the pursuer's teeth clamped on my thighs. Nor is it only external foes that threaten me, there are also some within the earth itself. I have never seen them, but I have heard stories about them, and I firmly believe in their existence. These are creatures from within the earth; not even legend can describe them, even their victims can barely have seen them; they come, you hear the scratch of their claws just below you in the ground, which is their element, and already you are lost. It makes no difference here that you are in your home, because it's really their dwelling. My exit will not save me from them, as it probably wouldn't save me under any circumstances, but rather ruin me; still, it remains a source of hope, and I am unable to live without it.

Apart from that one main highway, I am connected to the outside world by other, very narrow, fairly harmless byways, which keep me provided with breathable air. They are the work of forest voles and I have cleverly incorporated them into my overall design. They offer me the opportunity of sniffing the air some way off, and thus afford me further protection; also they are conduits for all sorts of small creatures which I eat up, so that I enjoy a certain modest amount of game, sufficient to keep body and soul together, without even having to leave my burrow, which of course is a considerable asset.

The most delightful aspect of the burrow, though, is its silence—a deceptive silence, admittedly, one that can suddenly be broken, and then all bets are off, but for the time being it still endures. I can creep for hours on end through my passageways and hear nothing beyond the occasional rustle of some small creature which I can put a sudden stop to with my teeth, or the trickling of some loose soil that serves to indicate the timeliness of some repair or other—otherwise all is silence. The forest air blows in, it's simultaneously warm and cool; sometimes I lie down and roll around in a passage for the sheer joy of it. It's a fine thing to have such a burrow as old age approaches, to have a roof over one's head as the autumn begins.

Every hundred yards or so I widen out the passageways to little round plazas, where I can comfortably curl up, warm myself, and rest. There I sleep the sweet sleep of peace, of assuaged appetite, of an objective attained, of home ownership. I don't know whether it's an atavistic instinct or whether the perils of even this edifice are still such as to rouse me, but periodically I wake up in panic out of a deep sleep, listen to the silence, which day and night never varies, smile with relief, and lapse back with limbs relaxed into a still deeper sleep. Poor vagrants, without a home, on the roads, in the forests, at best finding temporary refuge in a pile of leaves or amongst a horde of fellow creatures, exposed to the full vindictiveness of heaven and earth! While I lie here in a plaza secured in every direction—I have more than fifty of them in my burrow—and between drowsing and profound unconsciousness I pass the hours that I select for the purpose.

Not quite at the heart of the burrow, well selected for the eventuality of extreme danger, perhaps not of pursuit, but certainly of a siege is my central plaza. While everything else may be the work more of a concentrated mind than body, this citadel is in all its parts the product of the very hardest manual labor. Several times extreme physical exhaustion almost led me to abandon the task; I rolled on my back and cursed the project, dragged myself outside and left the burrow untenanted. I could afford to do so, seeing as I had no intention of returning to it, until, hours or even days later, I ruefully returned to it, almost raising a hymn on finding the structure intact, and joyfully resumed my labors. The work on the citadel was more difficult than it had to be, by which I mean that the burrow as a whole did not benefit from it; it was simply that the earth at the place where I had decided to situate my citadel happened to be very loose and sandy and needed to be pounded down, to create a large, beautiful curved surface. I spent whole days and nights ramming my forehead thousands of times into the soil, I was happiest when bloodied, because that meant the walls were beginning to acquire firmness, and so, as may be conceded, I earned the rights to my citadel.

In this citadel I keep my provisions: everything I manage to hunt down within the burrow that exceeds my immediate demands, and also everything I bring back from outside is piled up here. The citadel is so spacious that half a year's supplies do not fill it. This enables me to keep my holdings nicely spread out, so that I can walk up and down among them, play with them, rejoice at their quantity and their various odors, and retain an overall sense of what is what. Then I can always make adjustments and, according to the season, make the necessary advance calculations and foraging plans. There are times when I am so abundantly catered for that, out of indifference toward food, I don't lay a finger on the small fry that like to scuttle around here, though that may be incautious for other reasons. Because I am so regularly preoccupied with defensive preparations, my views regarding the exploitation of the burrow for such purposes are subject to constant revision, though within narrow parameters. Then it will seem to me to be asking for trouble to base the defenses entirely around the citadel: the extension of the burrow offers similarly extensive possibilities, and it seems more in accord with prudence to keep my provisions a little spread out, and to keep various smaller plazas stocked with them; and then I will decree that every third plaza is to be a reserve storage depot, or every fourth one a principal depot and every second one an auxiliary depot, and so on and so forth. Or I will keep some pathways clear— for reasons of deception—of the piles of supplies, or I will make spontaneous selections of a mere handful of plazas, purely according to their position vis-à-vis the exit. Every successive plan entails much onerous lifting work; I need to make the calculations and then carry the goods back and forth. Of course I can do so in my own sweet time, without undue haste, and it's not such a hardship to carry the good things in one's mouth, stop for a rest when one feels like it, and have a nibble of whatever happens to take one's fancy. What's worse are certain times, usually when I wake in panic, when it seems to me that the current disposition is wholly mistaken, fraught with danger, and needs to be instantly corrected, without regard to my general fatigue and exhaustion, because then I will hurry, then I will fly, because I have no time to make any calculations as I move to execute some carefully honed new plan. I grab randomly what I can between my teeth, drag, lug, sigh, groan, stumble, until some chance shift in my prevailing, excessively dangerous state of mind puts a stop to this, and I gradually come round, sober sense returns, and I barely understand my overhastiness. Then I inhale deeply the peace of my home that I have myself disturbed, return to my sleeping place, fall asleep on the spot in new-won exhaustion, and when I wake find I have as incontrovertible proof of my almost dreamlike night's work, a rat or something hanging from my teeth. Then there are other times when the siting of all provisions in one place is the way to go. What use to me are the supplies in little out-of-the-way plazas, how much is it even possible to store there, however much I take, it will only get in the way and perhaps even obstruct me in my effort either to defend myself or else to run away. Moreover, it's a foolish but true fact that one's morale suffers when one cannot see all one's stockpiles in one place, taking in at a glance what one has. Is it not possible, too, for things to get lost in the course of constant moving? I can't forever be galloping along my cross-passageways and rat-runs to see that everything is in proper order. The basic idea of a distribution of supplies may be correct, but really only when one has several sites at one's disposal like my citadel. Several such sites! If only! But who could build on such a scale? Also, it would be impossible retrospectively to integrate them in the overall plan.

I will admit that this is a flaw in the design, just as it is always a flaw to have no more than one of anything. And I concede too, that during the original construction, I had a dim sense, though clear enough when I thought about it, that on some level I had a yen for a plurality of citadels; I didn't give into it, I didn't feel up to such an enormous task; yes, I felt too weak even to imagine the required labor, and somehow consoled myself with other feelings no less vague that what would ordinarily not be sufficient, would in my own exceptional case, by special grace, be so, probably because providence had a particular interest in the preservation of my steamhammer brow. And so it is that I have only the one citadel, while the vague feelings that this one of all would this time be sufficient—they no longer exist. With things as they are, I must needs content myself with the one, the little plazas can't possibly replace it, and so I then begin again, when the feeling has grown in me, to drag everything back out of the little plazas to my citadel. For a little while then, it's a great comfort to me to have all the passageways and nodal points free, to watch the quantities of meat once again piling up in the citadel, wafting out to the outermost passageways their mingled odors which delight me as I stand far away identifying their respective provenances. Outstandingly peaceful times have often followed, in which slowly and step by step I move my sleeping sites back from the outer periphery to the interior, diving deeper into the world of the odors, until I can no longer stand it, and one night I charge to the citadel, conduct a massive clean-up operation, and gorge myself to the point of utter insensibility on the best things I have. Happy days, but dangerous, and anyone with the ability to exploit them could easily destroy me at little risk to themselves. Here too, the want of a second or third citadel makes itself felt, as it is the great and singular accumulation of provisions that undoes me. I seek variously to protect myself—the allocation of foods to the smaller plazas being one such stratagem—unfortunately, like the other strategies, it leads through privation to even greater rapacity, which overpowers my logical mind and leads me to make unwarranted changes to the overall defenses.

After such episodes, I tend to review the burrow in a bid to pull myself together, and after the needful repairs have been effected, I will often leave it altogether, if only for a brief stretch. The punishment of being gone for long seems to me too harsh, though I accept the need for occasional absences. There is always a certain feeling of formality when I approach the exit. During periods of domesticity I tend not to go there, even avoiding the upper reaches of the passageway altogether, nor is it at all easy to wander about there, because of the crazy zigzag of passageways I laid out; that was where my burrow began, back when I had little hope of ever fully realizing my blueprints, so I began almost a little whimsically, and the early pleasure I took in the work found expression in a labyrinth that at the time seemed to me the crown of all edifices, but which I deem today, probably more correctly, as a rather baroque bit of decoration, not really up to the standard of the whole thing, though perhaps amusing enough when viewed independently—here, make yourselves at home, I liked to quip to my invisible foes, and thought of them all choking to death in the initial labyrinth—but in reality it was no more than a rickety bit of ornamentation that would hardly be able to withstand a serious onslaught or a foe desperately struggling for his life.

Should I therefore rebuild it? I keep postponing the decision, and expect it will probably stay the way it is. Apart from the labor it would entail, it would also be about the most dangerous project one could imagine; at the time I embarked on the burrow, I was able to work there relatively undisturbed, the risk was not appreciably greater than any other time, whereas today it would amount to almost wantonly alerting the whole world to the existence of my burrow; today it's no longer possible. I am almost glad about this, a certain sentimental regard for this first example of my handiwork is of course also a factor. Besides, if a great attack should come, what style of entrance would save me? An entrance can deceive, distract, torment an attacker, and this one does some of all three. But a really concerted attack is something I would have to seek to oppose immediately with all the resources of the burrow as a whole and all the forces of my body and soul—just to state the obvious. So let the entrance stay the way it is. The burrow has so many naturally occurring weaknesses anyway, let it also keep this one that was all my own work, as I have belatedly but now all too well come to recognize. All this is, of course, not to say that I'm not occasionally, or even permanently, disquieted by this weakness. If I avoid this section of the burrow in the course of my wanderings, then it is principally because its aspect is disagreeable to me; I don't always care to be confronted by visible evidence of a shortcoming of the burrow when such shortcomings are too much present in my awareness anyway. Even if the mistake up there at the entrance endures forever, I would like to be spared the sight of it for as long as I may. Even if I am only heading in the general direction of the exit, and whole plazas and passageways still separate me from it, I still have the sense I am entering into an atmosphere of great danger; it feels sometimes as though my fur were thinning out, as though I might be standing there stripped to my moulted flesh, and be at that moment greeted by the howls of my enemies. Yes, perhaps the mere fact of an exit is enough to precipitate such unhealthy feelings, it marks the limits of the protections of home, but it is also this specific entryway that pains me. Sometimes I dream I have converted it, rebuilt it radically, from the ground up, or down, rapidly, with a giant's strength, unnoticed by anyone, and now it is impregnable; and there is no sweeter sleep than on such nights, tears of joy and relief still glitter in the hairs of my beard when I awake from it.

I need to overcome the ordeal of this labyrinth when I go out, and then I find it both irritating and moving to get lost for a moment in my construction, and see the work still striving to justify its existence to me, even though my opinion of it was fixed long ago. But then I arrive under the moss cover, which I sometimes allow—that shows how long a period I don't leave my home for—to knit together with the forest floor, and now all that is needed is just a little bunt of the head, and I am out in the open. For a long time I forbear to make the required movement, and if I didn't have the labyrinth to negotiate, then who knows, I might just turn tail and go back inside. After all, why not? Your home is secure and well protected; you live in peace, are warm and well-fed, the master—sole master—of a multiplicity of passageways and plazas, and all that you are willing, if not to sacrifice, then at least to put at risk; you have every possibility of being able to reconquer it, but you agree to play a dangerous, even a madcap game with it. Are there any sensible reasons for doing so? No, there can be no sensible reasons for such a risk. But then I cautiously push open the trapdoor and I'm outside; I slowly let it fall back, and, as quickly as I can, sprint away from the telltale spot.

But I'm not really in the open—true, I'm no longer squeezing myself through the passageways, and instead am racing around the woods, feeling a surge of fresh strength in my limbs, for which the burrow seems to have, so to speak, no room, not even in the citadel, even if it were ten times its present size; also provisioning is better outside, hunting may be more difficult, and successes rarer, but the results are in every respect superior. I will deny none of this, and I appreciate it and enjoy it, at least as much as any other creature, and probably rather more, because I don't hunt in the manner of a vagrant, foolishly or desperately, but calmly and with a sense of purpose. I am not made for life out of doors or condemned to it, because I know my time there is limited. I can't hunt around there forever, but when I am ready, so to speak, and tired of the upper life, I will be summoned by someone whose invitation I am unable to refuse. And so I am able to make the most of my time there, or rather I could or should have been able to, only I can't. I am preoccupied with my burrow. I rush away from the exit, but it's not long before I'm back there. I look for a good observation post, from where I survey the entrance to my dwelling—this time from outside—for entire days and nights. Call me foolish, but doing so gives me deep satisfaction and even reassurance. I have the feeling then that I am not standing in front of my dwelling, but rather in front of my sleeping self, as though I had the good fortune to be at one and the same time fast asleep and to keep a vigilant eye on myself. I am, so to speak, set apart, permitted to see the shapes of night not only in the helplessness and trust of sleep, but to meet them in reality fully alert and with the calm judgment of one awake. And I find then that in an odd way I am not so badly off as I was inclined to think and probably will think again when I climb down into my abode. In this respect—and probably in others as well, but certainly in this one—my excursions are truly invaluable. Yes, however deliberately I built my entrance off to the side—where the overall plan imposed certain constraints—the footfall there, on the basis of say a week's observations, is very great, but perhaps that's the case in all inhabited areas, and it may well be better to be exposed to more footfall, which, by sheer press of numbers is more likely to carry on past, than to be exposed in eremitic isolation to a single diligently searching intruder. Here there are many foes and still more enemy supporters, but they get in each other's way and in their distractedness go chasing past my burrow. I have never seen anyone actually nosing around the entrance, to my joy and no doubt theirs too, because mad with anxiety, I would certainly have hurled myself at their throats. And then there were others who came close whom I did not dare to interfere with, and from whom, if I so much as sensed them in the distance, I would have been compelled to flee; I oughtn't really to express myself with any degree of confidence regarding their behavior vis-à-vis my burrow, but it is probably enough to reassure me that I returned shortly afterward, found none of them there any-more and my entrance undamaged. There were happy times in which I could almost tell myself that the world had ceased or at least relaxed its opposition to me, or that the mighty scale of the burrow had taken me out of the struggle for sur-vival that had been mine until then. The burrow perhaps af-fords more protection than I thought, or that, when inside it, I dared to suppose. It went so far that I sometimes had the childish wish never to return to it, but to settle down some-where near the entrance, to spend my life observing the en-trance, and to concentrate and to find my happiness in the sure way the burrow—had I been inside it—would have kept me safe. Well, one often awakes in panic from childish dreams. What kind of protection did I think I might be ob-serving? Is it even possible to judge the degree of danger in the burrow on the basis of what I experience whilst outside it? Are my foes able to perceive anything properly when I'm not in the burrow? Yes, they will have some awareness of me, but not full awareness. And isn't the sense of full perception what one needs to judge normal dangers? So these are only partial or semi-experiments I am conducting here, calculated to afford me relief, only for their false reassurance to lay me open to greater dangers. No, I'm not watching over my own sleep, as I thought I was; rather, I'm the one who's asleep, while my destroyer awaits. Perhaps he is among those who casually stroll past the entrance, just making sure, as I do, that the door is still intact and awaiting attack, strolling past because they know perfectly well that the master is not within or even that he is lurking in the shrubbery not far away. And I leave my observation post and feel fed up with life in the open; I feel that being here has nothing more to teach me, not now and not later. And I feel very much inclined to say goodbye to everything here, to climb down into my burrow and never come out again, let things take whatever course they will, and not try to delay them by any more useless observations. But spoiled by the fact that I've been allowed to watch everything that was happening by the entrance for such a long time, it feels particularly tormenting to go through the really eye-catchingly conspicuous procedure of descent and not to know what is going on behind my back, much less what will happen once the trapdoor has closed behind me. First I make trial runs on stormy nights, rapidly throwing down my prey—that appears to work, but whether it actually works will only be revealed once I have climbed down myself; it will become apparent—though not to me, or if to me, then only once it is too late. So I desist from that, and don't climb down myself. I dig, of course, at a suitable distance from the actual entrance, a trial hole, no wider than I am, and also sealed off by a layer of moss. I creep into that hole, cover it over after me, wait through carefully calculated shorter and longer intervals at various times of day, then throw off the layer of moss, come out and make my observations. My experiences are very varied, both good and bad, there seems to be no general law or infallible method of climbing in. As a result I am both grateful not to have climbed into the actual entrance and frantic because I will soon have to. I am not a million miles from the decision to go right away, to take up the old cheerless life that offered no security whatever, that was nothing but an unending string of perils with each individual danger correspondingly impossible to identify and to counter, as the contrast between my secure burrow and the rest of life continually teaches me. Of course, a decision like that would be complete folly, produced by too much time spent meaninglessly at large; still, the burrow is mine, I have only to take one or two steps and I will be in safety. And then I break free of all my doubts and make a beeline for the door in plain daylight, determined to raise it up; but I somehow can't do it, I run past it, and deliberately fling myself into a thorn bush in order to mortify myself, to punish myself for a fault I can't identify. Because in the end I have to tell myself that I was right and that it really is impossible to descend without exposing the dearest thing I have to all around, for at least a moment—on the ground, in the trees, in the air. And the danger is not imaginary, it's very real. It doesn't have to be an actual foe that I provoke to follow me; it can perfectly well be a little innocent, some repulsive little female, pursuing me out of curiosity and so, without knowing it, becoming the leader of the world against me. It doesn't have to be that either, perhaps it's—and this is no better than the other; in some respects it's the very worst—perhaps it's someone of my own sort, an expert in burrows, some denizen of the forest, a lover of peace, but also an uncouth savage who wants to be housed without going to the trouble of building anything. If only he would come now, if only he discovered my entrance with his filthy greed, if only he started working on it, lifting up the moss; if only he could do it, if he were to swiftly shoulder his way in, and was already in so far that only his behind for a moment was still visible—then at last I could run at him; free of all concerns I could leap at him, bite him, rend his flesh, chew it, and drain his blood and cram his carcass down there with the rest of the quarry; above all, though, and this is the main thing, I could be back in my burrow, and this time happy to admire the labyrinth, first of all, however, pulling the cover of moss shut after me, to rest, I think, for what remained of my life. But no one comes, and I am still dependent on myself. Constantly obsessed with the difficulty of the maneuver, I lose much of my timidity, I no longer physically avoid the entrance, I start circling around it, it's become my favorite occupation, almost as though I was the enemy now, exploring the best opportunity to stage a successful break-in. If only I had someone I could trust, whom I could set in my observation post, then I could calmly make my descent. I would arrange for my ally to observe the scene during my descent and for a long time after, and, in case of any signs of danger, to tap on the moss cover, or not as the case may be. Then everything above me and behind me would be tickety-boo, there would be nothing left—or just my trusted ally. Because if he doesn't ask for anything in return, not so much as a tour of the burrow, and even that—willingly admitting someone into the burrow is something I would find extremely difficult; I built it for myself, not for visitors—I think I would refuse; even at the price that he would make it possible for me to get into the burrow, I think I wouldn't admit him. But how could I admit him anyway, because then either I would have to let him go in by himself, which is beyond imagining, or we would have to go down together, which would annul the advantage he is supposed to give me—that of making his observations when I am in. And what about trust? The fellow I put my trust in when I look him in the eye, can I trust him as much when the moss is between us and I can no longer see him? It's relatively easy to trust someone when you have him under observation, or at least are in a position to observe him; perhaps it's even possible to trust someone at a distance, but to trust someone on the outside from within the burrow, and so from within a different world, that I think is impossible. But who needs such doubts; it's enough to think of all the innumerable pitfalls that, during or after my descent, could prevent my confidant from fulfilling his duty, and the incalculable consequences for me of even the most minor hitch. No, taking everything together, I shouldn't even lament the fact that I am alone, and have no one I can trust. I am sure that costs me no advantage, and it probably saves me from some harm. Trust is only to be placed in myself and the burrow. I should have thought about that sooner, and made some arrangements for the contingency that is currently preoccupying me. It would have been at least partly possible at the inception of the building. I should have designed the first passageway in such a way that it had two entrances at a suitable distance from one another, so that I could have entered in one place with the inevitable palaver, quickly crossed to the second entrance, lifted the moss there—which would have to have been adapted a little to the purpose—and spent a couple of days and nights on the qui vive. That's the only way it could have been right; of course two entrances means a doubling of the risk, but that consideration would have had to be quelled particularly as one of the entrances, which would only have been conceived as an observation point, could have been kept very narrow. And with that I lose myself in technical deliberations, and I start to dream my old dream of the perfect burrow again; that calms me down a little; enraptured and with eyes closed I imagine distinct and less distinct architectural features to enable me to slip in and out unobserved.

As I lie there thinking, I rate these features very highly, but only as technical accomplishments, not as real advantages, because what, when it comes down to it, is the point of this unhindered slipping in and out? It all points to an unquiet mind, an uncertain sense of self, unclean appetites, bad habits, which will all become much worse in view of the burrow that is standing there, capable of imbuing me with peace, if only I open myself to it wholly. Now of course I am outside, and seeking a possibility of reentering it, that's where technical modifications would indeed be very desirable. In my present state of anxiety I tend to underestimate the burrow, seeing it merely as a hole in the ground, to be crawled into as safely as possible. Of course, it is such a hole, or ought to be, and if I merely imagine I am beset with dangers, then with gritted teeth and all the willpower at my command, I want the burrow to be nothing but a hole designed for my salvation, and that it might fulfill this clearly set task to the greatest degree possible, and I don't greatly mind what else it is or can be. But the situation is that in reality—that reality for which in moments of panic one has little sense, and even in tranquil times, it is a perspective that takes some acquiring—it may afford considerable security, but not enough, for do one's worries ever quite stop when in it? They are other, prouder, more substantial, often greatly repressed worries, but their consuming effect is perhaps the same as those worries that life outside affords. If I had only conceived the burrow for my personal security, then I would not have been cheated, but the relationship between my vast labor and any actual security, at least inasmuch as I am able to feel it and profit from it, would not be a favorable one from my point of view. It's a painful admission to make, but it has to be done, particularly in view of the entrance over there, which seems to seal itself against me, the builder and owner—yes, positively to be clamped shut. But that's the thing: the burrow isn't just a hole to dive into! When I'm standing in the citadel, surrounded by my towering stocks of meat, facing the ten exits that radiate from there, each one fulfilling its role in the overall plan, going up or down, straight or curved, widening or narrowing, and all equally silent and empty and ready, each one after its fashion all set, to lead me on to the numerous plazas, and these too all of them empty and silent—then I have little thought of security, then I know exactly that this is my castle, which I carved out of the recalcitrant earth by scratching and biting, stamping and butting, my castle that can never belong to another in any way, that is so much mine that in the end I can take the mortal wound from my foe quite calmly, because my blood will drain away into my soil, and will not go to waste. And, other than this, what is the point of the lovely hours that I like to spend half peacefully asleep, half joyfully awake in my passageways, these passageways that are so nicely adapted for my personal use, for luxurious stretching, for childish rolling around, for dreamily lying there and then blissfully dropping off to sleep and the little plazas, for all their uniformity of appearance, each one well known to me, each one effortlessly identified by the curve of its walls, they enfold me peacefully and warmly, as no nest enfolds a bird. And all—all!—silent and empty.

But if that's the case, what am I hesitating for, why am I more afraid of the intruder than of the possibility that I may perhaps never see inside my burrow again? Well, this last is happily an impossibility, I have no need to rationalize what the burrow means to me, I and the burrow belong together in such a way that I could calmly, perfectly calmly, for all my fears, settle here, not even seeking to persuade myself to open the entrance; it would be absolutely enough if I were to wait here idly, because in the long run nothing can separate us, so certain am I that I will descend there again. But how much time may pass until then, and how many things can happen in that time, here as much as down there? And it's purely up to me to try and reduce that period of time, and to do the requisite thing right away.

And now, unable to think for tiredness, with shambling legs and head hanging, half asleep, more groping than walking, I go over to the entrance, slowly lift the moss, slowly climb down; out of sheer distraction I leave the entrance uncovered for an unnecessarily long time, but then call myself to order, climb back up to make amends, but then why climb up? It's only the moss cover that needs to be pulled shut—all right—so I climb back down, and now at last I pull the moss cover shut. It's the only way I can settle this thing, in such a state. Then I lie under the moss on top of the quarry I've dropped, bathed in blood and meat juices, and finally begin to sleep the longed-for sleep. Nothing is bothering me, no one has followed me, above the moss things at least appear to be peaceful and even if it weren't so, I am past the stage of being able to observe; I have changed places, I have returned to my burrow from the upper world, and I feel the effect immediately. It's a new world that gives me fresh strength; whatever in the upper world felt like tiredness doesn't apply here. I have come home from a journey, crazed with tiredness, but the reunion with my old premises, the settling-in activities that await me, the need to give all the rooms at least a superficial inspection, but above all to go through to the citadel—all that transforms my tiredness into restlessness and enthusiasm, it's as though during the moment of my reentering the burrow I had taken a long and restorative nap. The initial work is very laborious and claims me utterly: getting the quarry through the narrow and thin-walled passages of the labyrinth. I press forward with all my strength, and I am making headway, but progress is far too slow; to speed things up, I tear off some of the mass of flesh and force my way past the rest, shuffle through it, now I have just a little bit in front of me, now it's easier to transport, but I am caught in the middle of my meat supplies here in the narrow passageways that I don't always find it easy to get through when unencumbered, I could even asphyxiate in my own provisions, sometimes I can only keep them at bay by guzzling and swilling them down. But I get through, I make reasonable time, the labyrinth is negotiated; sighing with relief, I stand in one of the standard-gauge passageways, bundle the quarry down a rat-run into a main passage steeply sloping down to the main plaza, designed for just such eventualities. Now my labor's over, the whole kit and caboodle rolls and trickles down almost by itself. Finally back in my citadel! All is unchanged, no major calamities seem to have happened, such minor damage as I take in at a glance will be put right in no time. But first I have to face the long wanderings through the passageways, but that's no effort, that's like chatting with friends, just as I did in the old days, or—I'm not that old, but my memory for some things has dimmed—as I did or heard of others doing in the old days. I start out deliberately slowly on the second passageway; after inspecting the citadel I have endless time, whenever I am in the burrow I have endless time, because everything I do there is good and important and, if you like, sustaining. I start out on the second passageway, then break off the inspection halfway, cross to the third passageway and follow it back to the citadel, and now I need to take the second passageway again, and I'm toying with the work, and adding to it and laughing to myself and delighting in it and my head is spinning with all the work, but I don't stop. It's for your sake, you passageways and plazas and above all you, my citadel, that I've come here, setting my life at nothing after trembling over it for so long from sheer stupidity, merely postponing my return. What do I care now about danger, since I'm with you? You belong to me, I belong to you, we're together, what can happen to us? Even if the creatures up above are milling around, and their snouts are itching to push through the moss. With its silence and emptiness the burrow welcomes me back and echoes what I say. But now I am overcome by a certain lassitude and roll myself up in one of my favorite plazas; I still haven't inspected everything by a long way, I want to finish the inspection; I have no thought of sleeping here, I've just given into the temptation to stop here for a moment as if I was going to sleep, I want to see if I can still do it like before. Well, it seems I can, but I'm not able to rouse myself, I stay here, fast asleep. I must have been sleeping for a very long time. I am only just waking from the last cycle of sleep; it must have been a very light sleep, because the thing that has awakened me is a barely audible hissing. I straightaway understand that the small fry, far too little attended to by me, have tunneled some new path while I was away, their path has encountered another, older one, the two airs have collided and produced the hissing sound. What an assiduous crowd they are, and how irksome in their industry! By listening carefully at the walls of my passageways and undertaking trial drillings, I will have to establish the site of the disturbance, and then deal with the noise. Incidentally, the fresh tunnel, if it somehow chimes with the form of the burrow, may come in handy as a new supplemental airshaft. But I mean to pay more attention to the little things from now on; I won't spare a single one.

Since I have extensive practice with such investigations, it probably won't take me very long, and I can begin right away—yes, I have other work waiting for me, but this is the most urgent task—I require silence in my passageways. This particular sound is relatively innocent; I didn't even hear it at first, even though it will have been present already; I had to be fully reacclimatized to hear it, if you like, it's a sound that requires the hearing of the owner-occupier doing his proper job. And it's not even constant, as such sounds tend to be, there are long breaks in it, evidently a function of occasional blockages in the airflow. So I commence my investigations, but I am not able to find the right spot to intervene; I start a few random excavations, of course nothing turns up, and the great labor of digging and the still greater labor of filling in and making good is all in vain. I don't even succeed in coming any closer to the source of the sound: it continues reedily at regular intervals, sometimes like hissing, sometimes more like whistling. I could ignore it for the time being; I do find it terribly disruptive, but there is little doubt as to its presumed source, so it will hardly grow any louder; on the contrary, it's been known—admittedly, I've hardly ever cared to wait that long—for such sounds to disappear by themselves over time owing to the further efforts of the little burrowers; and that aside, some chance event often leads one along the trail of the disturbance, while more systematic investigation can turn up nothing for long periods. So I comfort myself, and would rather wander through the passageways and visit the plazas, many of which I have not yet revisited, and in between times treat myself to periodic visits to the citadel; but it won't let go of me, I am compelled to go on looking. A lot of time, a lot of time, time for which I have better uses, is taken up by the little folk. On these occasions, it is usually the technical difficulty that attracts me. I imagine, for instance, based on the sound that my ear from long experience is able to analyze minutely, in scrupulous detail, the exact cause and then I am compelled to check whether the reality bears any relation to it. With good reason, because without a positive identification I am unable to feel safe, even if it's just a matter of knowing which way a grain of sand will go as it rolls down a surface. A noise like that is by no means unimportant in such a context. But important or not, and try as I may, I find nothing, or rather, I find too much. It had to happen in my favorite plaza, I think to myself, and I go far away from it, almost halfway to the next plaza; the whole thing is a joke really, as though I wanted to prove that it wasn't my favorite plaza that has disappointed me, but that the disturbances are elsewhere, and smiling, I set myself to listen; then, I kid you not, I hear the same hissing sound here as well. It's nothing; sometimes I think no one but me would be capable of hearing it; admittedly, with my practiced ear, I am hearing it ever more distinctly, even though in reality it's exactly the same sound, as I can tell by making the comparison. Nor does it get any louder, as I can tell by leaving the wall and standing in the middle of the passage and listening. It takes considerable concentration, even immersion, to pick up the ghost of a sound, which is more guessed at than actually heard. But it's this constant volume all around that I find most disturbing because it won't permit itself to be reconciled with my original assumption. If I had correctly guessed the source of the noise, then it should have been loudest from a specific place that I would have had to discover, and then be diminishing from there. But if my explanation wasn't correct, what else could it be? There remained the possibility that there were two centers of the sound, that I had thus far picked up equally distant from both of them, and that as I approached one, the volume from it would increase, but by simultaneously decreasing as I left the other one, the overall volume remained more or less constant. I almost thought that, when I listened intently, I could hear differences in quality that bore out the new hypothesis, though these were extremely hard to make out. At any rate, I would have to greatly extend the area of my operations. So I follow the passage down to the citadel and start to listen there. Curious, it was the same sound here as well. Now it's a sound produced by the digging of some inconsequential animals that have made use of my absence to get up to no good; at any rate there is no question of any threat to myself, they are preoccupied with their work, and so long as they encounter no obstruction, they will carry on in the same direction; I know all that, but even so it baffles me and excites me and confuses the faculties I need for my work that they have dared to penetrate as far as the citadel. In that respect I'm not interested in any distinctions: was it the considerable depth at which the citadel is located, was it its great extension and the corresponding strong movement of air, which frightened the diggers, or was it simply the fact that it was the citadel—the absolute grandeur of the place— that had got through to their dull wits by some agency or other? Thus far at least I had not observed any excavations touching the walls of the citadel. Animals sometimes came here, in numbers, drawn by the powerful exudations; this actually is where I had some of my best hunting, but they usually dug their way in somewhere up above, struck a passageway, and came down it—sheepishly maybe, but powerfully attracted nonetheless. Whereas now they were apparently coming through the walls. If only I had managed to follow through on the grand plans of my youth and early manhood, or if only I had had the strength to carry them out, because it wasn't that I lacked the willpower. It was one of my most cherished plans to seal off the citadel from the soil around, walling it in but only to a thickness roughly corresponding to my own height, and above that to create a hollow space—on a narrow foundation unfortunately not entirely separable from the soil—going all around the citadel. This hollow space I had imagined—and surely rightly—would have provided the most beautiful accommodation I could ever have had. To dangle on the curve, to pull myself up, to slither down, to turn somersaults and once again feel the ground under my feet, and all these games literally on the body of the citadel, though not in its actual confines; to be able to avoid the citadel, to allow my eyes to relax from it, to put off the joy of seeing it again to some future time, and yet not to be away from it, but to have it literally in my grasp, something that is impossible if one has nothing but the humdrum open approach to it; and above all to be able to guard it, to be so amply compensated for the inability to see it that certainly, had there been a choice between remaining in the citadel or the hollow, then certainly you would have chosen the hollow space for the rest of your days, always promenading up and down there, protecting the citadel. Then there would be no noises in the walls, no impertinent digging up to its purlieus, then peace would be guaranteed, and I would be its guarantor, I wouldn't be listening, nauseated, to the scrabbling of small fry, but with rapture to something I totally miss: the sound of silence over the citadel.

But none of this beauty exists, and I need to go about my work; I should be almost glad that the citadel is involved, because that will lend me wings. It increasingly appears that I will need all my strength for what at first seemed a rather modest task. I listen attentively now to the walls of the citadel and wherever I press my ear, high and low, to the walls or to the ground, at the entrances or deep within, everywhere I hear the same sound. And how much time, how much concentration goes on picking up this sporadic sound.

If you want, you can take some little comfort from the fact that here in the citadel, as opposed to the passageways, if you take your ear off the ground, you hear nothing—that's a function of the dimensions of the citadel. It's only to rest, to bring myself back to reality that I periodically undertake these trials, and then I'm happy when I hear nothing. What's happened, after all? My first attempts at an explanation totally failed in the face of this phenomenon. But then I must quickly reject other accounts that present themselves. You might suppose that what I am hearing is the small fry at work. But that would fly in the face of all experience; something I have never heard before, that was always present—I can't suddenly overnight have begun to hear it. My sensitivity to disturbances in the burrow has perhaps become more acute over the years, but my actual hearing can't have become keener. It's in the nature of the little creatures that one doesn't hear them, or else I would never have tolerated them; at the risk of starving, I would have exterminated them. But maybe—I have a sneaking suspicion—this is some animal I am unacquainted with. It's a possibility; of course I've observed the forms of life here below minutely and for a long time, but the world is varied, and one is never short of nasty surprises. It couldn't be a single specimen, there would have to be a major herd of them that had suddenly moved into my territory, a major herd of small animals, that, since they are at least audible, must be larger than the small fry, if not by much, since the noise of their labor is still quite faint. So they could be animals unknown, a migratory herd moving through, disturbing me, yes, but not here for very long. I could wait it out, and avoid doing unnecessary work. But if they are new animals, why is it I have yet to see them? I have undertaken much digging to try and nab one of them, but I haven't succeeded. It occurs to me that they might be really tiny creatures, much smaller than the varieties known to me, and that the only considerable aspect of them is the noise they make. I go back through my spoils, toss the lumps of soil up in the air to break them up into tiny bits, but I find no trace of the noisemakers. It dawns on me gradually that these random excavations are not the way to go; I will end up tunneling through the walls of my burrow, scraping up something here and there, but not taking the time to repair the cavities; already, many places have heaps of earth blocking the path and the view. I may find it only marginally upsetting that I can neither walk around nor look nor rest, and often I find I've nodded off over my work in some hole or other, one paw clawed into the soil I wanted to pull a piece out of with the last of my energy. I will change my methods. I will construct a wide trench in the direction of the noise, and not stop digging until, regardless of my theorizing, I have succeeded in finding the true source of the noise. Then if it is in my power, I will deal with it, and if not, I shall at least have some certainty. This certainty will bring me either calm or turmoil, but whichever it is, there will be no doubt about it and it will be justified. This resolution does me good: everything I've done so far strikes me as having been overhasty, attributable to the excitement of returning home, not yet free of the alarms of the upper world, and not yet fully reabsorbed into the tranquility of the burrow; still oversensitized by having gone without it for so long, I have allowed myself to be utterly distracted by a new and admittedly remarkable phenomenon. So what is it? A gentle hiss, only audible at long intervals, nothing at all really, you might get used to it, well, maybe not that, but you could be content merely to observe it for a while, give it a watching brief, i.e. listen in every few hours or so and patiently note the results, but not do as I did and rub your ear along the walls, and scratch open the ground almost every time you pick up the sound, to no end, other than to express your inner disquiet. That's all about to change now, I hope. And then again, I don't hope—as I admit to myself with eyes closed, furious with myself—because I am trembling with this agitation every bit as much as I was hours ago, and if common sense didn't hold me back, I would probably just start digging somewhere else, regardless of whether I heard anything there or not—dully, stubbornly, just for the sake of digging, not so very different from the small fry that digs for no reason, or only because they eat the soil. My sensible new plan both tempts me and doesn't. There are no objections to it, at least I know of none; it is bound, as I see it, to lead to a result. And all the same, at some level I don't trust it, I have so little faith in it that I am not even alarmed by the possible terrors of what it may ultimately turn up, I don't even believe in the terror; yes, it seems to me that from the very first appearance of the noise, I had thought of such a purposeful excavation, and the only reason I didn't embark on it was because I had no confidence in it.

Of course I will begin to dig such a trench: I have no choice; but not right away, I will put off the work a little, until common sense has returned to me, I won't plunge into it. First I'll make good the damage I've done to the burrow with my scrabbling around; that will take some time, but it's important; the new trench will in all probability be long if it does actually get anywhere, and if it leads nowhere, it will be positively unending; at any rate that work will require a longer period of absence from the burrow, not so much maybe as lately in the upper world, and I can break off the work when I feel like it and go on visits home; and even if I don't, the air from the citadel will still waft across to me, and accompany me while on the job, but it still entails a period of absence from the burrow proper and the surrender to an uncertain destiny, so let me at least ensure that I leave the burrow in good order; I don't want it to appear that in fighting for my peace and quiet, I ended up destroying it and leaving it derelict. So I begin scraping the soil back into the holes, work I know intimately, I've done it thousands of times almost without feeling that it was a job at all, and that, especially as regards the final pressing down and smoothing out—this is not patting myself on the back, it's the simple truth—I am a past master at. This time, though, it feels hard, I'm absentminded, I keep stopping to press my ear to the wall to listen, indifferently letting pawfuls of earth I've just hoisted up trickle back down the slope. The final cosmetic improvements, which call for heightened concentration, are almost beyond me. Ugly bulges are left, unsightly cracks, not to mention the fact that overall it's impossible to give a patched piece of wall any of the old elan. I try to console myself by saying it's just a provisional job. When I'm back, once peace has been restored, I can give it a proper professional going-over, and it will all be done in the twinkling of an eye. In fairy tales, things are forever being done in the twinkling of an eye, and this bit of consolation is no more than a fairy tale. It would be so much better to do the job properly now, much more practical than forever interrupting it, traipsing through the passages and identifying fresh places where I can hear the noise; which is actually terribly easy, because it involves nothing more than stopping pretty much anywhere at random and listening. And then I make further unhelpful discoveries. Sometimes it feels as though the noise has stopped—you remember there are long pauses—sometimes you can ignore a little hiss, because of the way the blood is throbbing in your ear, then two pauses merge into one, and for a while you imagine the hissing has stopped for good.

You stop listening, you leap up, life is turned upside down, it's as though a source has opened from where the silence of the burrow streams forth. You do anything rather than check your new discovery, you go looking for someone you confided it to unquestioned before, you race off to the citadel, you remember that with everything you are, you have awakened to a new life, that it's ages since you had anything to eat, you grab a handful of something from the now somewhat soiled provisions, and are still gulping it down as you run back to the place where you made your incredible discovery; at first you want nothing more than casually, fleetingly, while snacking, to hear it again, you cock an ear, but the merest half attention is enough to tell you that you've made a howling blunder, because there's the hissing again merrily in the distance. You spit out what's in your mouth and feel like treading it into the ground, and you go straight back to work, though you're not sure where to start, some place where something needs doing, and there's no shortage of those, so you mechanically get busy doing something, as if a foreman has arrived on site and you had to put on a bit of a show for him. But after you've been working in that style for some little time, you make your next discovery. The noise seems to have got louder, not much louder, of course, but distinctly louder, you can clearly hear it. And this sounding louder seems to suggest a coming closer, and much more clearly than you hear the louder sound, you seem to see the pace at which it is getting nearer. You recoil from the wall; you try to take in all the possible implications of this latest discovery. You have the feeling you never really put the burrow on any sort of proper defense footing; you meant to, of course, but contrary to all the lessons of life you thought the danger of an attack and hence the putting on a defense footing was remote, or if not remote (how could that be possible!), then at least less important than designing it for a peaceful life, which was what became your priority throughout the burrow. A lot of things could have been done in that other direction, without even changing the basic design, but over the years quite unaccountably it hasn't been done. I've been fortunate over all these years; luck made me its darling. I was uneasy, but unease within an overall context of good fortune doesn't matter.

The thing to do now, and urgently, would be to revisit the burrow with a view to its defense, imagine every conceivable defensive modality, then come up with a strategy and a concomitant schedule of work, and then straightaway embark on it, as fresh as a youngster. That would have been the thing, for which, as I say, it is too late, but that would have been what was needed, not all the digging of some kind of massive experimental trench that actually serves no purpose, which leaves me defenseless even as I put all my strength into seeking out the danger, as if it couldn't come along soon enough at its own speed. All of a sudden I no longer understand my own earlier plan, the once rational scheme seems to be wholly unreasonable; once again I drop my work and I stop listening too; I no longer want to come upon any more reinforcements; I've had enough of these discoveries; I drop everything; I would be perfectly happy if only I could succeed in resolving my own inner turmoil. Once again, I allow myself to be drawn away by my passages, I come to others, ever more

remote, that I have not seen since my return and are still un-
touched by my scrabbling claws, whose silence is roused by
my coming and settles over me. I don't surrender to it though,
I don't even know what I'm looking for, probably just to pass
the time. I wander around until I get to the labyrinth, I am
drawn to listen at the moss cover; these are the remote ob-
jects, remote at any rate for the time being, that hold my interest. I go up there and listen. Profound silence; how I love it,
no one disturbs my burrow here, everyone has his own business which has nothing to do with me, how ever did I manage
to get to this point? Here under the moss is now perhaps the
only place in my burrow where I can listen for hours and hear
nothing. A complete reversal, my vulnerable point has become a place of peace, while the citadel has been polluted by
the noise and perils of the world. And worse, even here there
is in reality no peace, nothing has changed, silent or rackety,
danger lurks just as it did above the moss, but I have become
insensitive to it, too much preoccupied with the hissing
within my walls. Am I overwhelmed by it? It grows louder, it
comes closer, but I wend my way through the labyrinth and
stop up here under the moss, it's almost as if I were leaving
the building to the hisser, happy just to have a little peace up
here. The hisser? Am I coming to a different and definitive
sense of the source of the noise? The noise surely comes from
the runnels dug by the small fry? Isn't that my settled opinion? I don't think I've departed from it. And if it doesn't come
directly from their runnels, then somehow it does so indi-
rectly. And if it should be nothing to do with them, then there
are no assumptions to be made, and one would have to wait
for the source to appear or to be found. One could even now
be toying with suppositions; it would be possible to say for
instance that a water leak must have happened far away, and

what I take to be a hissing or whistling is actually a rushing sound. But quite apart from the fact that I have no experience of this sort—the one time I stumbled upon ground water I immediately diverted it and it never came back in this sandy soil—apart from that it remains a hissing and is not to be misinterpreted as a rushing. But what good are all one's injunctions to remain calm: the imagination refuses to rest and I still insist on believing—pointless to deny it to oneself— that the hissing comes from an animal, not from many little ones, but a single big one. There are things that suggest otherwise: the fact that the sound may be heard from all over, and always at the same volume, and indifferently day and night. Of course, one's first assumption would be that there are many small animals, but since I surely would have encountered them in the course of my digging and haven't, what I am left with is the existence of a single large animal, especially as what seems to contradict this assumption are just things that don't rule that out, but merely make it dangerous beyond all imagining. That's the only reason I refused to credit this hypothesis. Now I will desist from this self-deception. For a long time I've toyed with the idea that the reason it can be heard a long way away is because it's working furiously, its progress through the soil is like a pedestrian's over the ground, the earth shakes all around its digging, even when it's passed through, this afterquake and the sound of its working are merged in the great distance, and I, hearing just the last ebbing away of the sound, hear it everywhere the same. What contributes to this is the fact that the animal is not heading toward me, which is why the noise doesn't change, rather it has a plan whose purpose I can't detect, but I have to assume that this animal—perhaps without even being aware of my existence—is encircling me, it has probably already traced several circles around my burrow since I first became aware of it. And now it seems the noise is getting louder, which means the circles are closing in. What gives me pause is the quality of the sound, the hissing or whistling. When I scrape and scratch at the soil in my way, it sounds very different. The only way I can account for the noise is by saying to myself that the principal tools of this animal are not its claws—though maybe they are used in some auxiliary way—but its snout or trunk, which, aside from its immense strength, evidently must have some kind of edge as well. Presumably it drills its trunk into the soil with a single mighty thrust and rips out a large piece of it, and all this time I hear nothing—this is during the pause—but then it draws breath for a fresh thrust, and this drawing of breath, which must be an earth-shattering sound, not just on account of the animal's brute strength, but also because of its haste, its zeal, this sound comes through to me as a soft hissing. What I remain unable to account for is its uninterrupted working, perhaps the rhythmic intervals allow it tiny rest periods, but it hasn't needed a substantial period of rest yet, day and night it digs, always equally fresh and strong, with its mind focused on the plan it wants to carry out, and for which it possesses all needful attributes. Now, I wasn't ready for such an opponent. But apart from its idiosyncratic qualities, all this just betokens something I always had cause to fear, and should always have made preparations for: someone is coming. How was it, I wonder, that things remained blissfully quiet for so long? Who so directed the paths of my opponents that they made great detours around my property? Why was I kept sheltered for so long, only to be so alarmed now? What were all those minor threats I spent my time thinking through, compared to this one! Did I hope, as owner of this burrow, to prevail against all comers? When, as owner of this great and sensitive work, I am truly defenseless against any serious attacker, when the joy of ownership has spoilt me, the burrow's vulnerability has rendered me vulnerable, its injuries hurt me as much as if they had been mine own. This is what I should have thought about in advance, not just my own defense—though how irresponsibly and inconsequentially I did that!—but that of the burrow. Care should have been exercised that individual parts of the burrow, and as many of these as possible, if they came under attack, should have been targeted by landslides that could be arranged at a moment's notice, to separate the attacker from the less exposed parts, and by using such quantities of earth and to such effect that the attacker would not even have guessed that the actual burrow still lay ahead of him. And more, these landslips should have been calculated not merely to conceal the burrow, but also to bury the assailant. And I didn't undertake the least step in this direction, I was childishly irresponsible, I spent my adult years with childish things; even the thought of danger to me was something to play with and I neglected to think about actual dangers. And there was no shortage of warnings either. Not admittedly anything on the scale of the present warnings, but still there was something similar during the infancy of the burrow. I was working then as a sort of junior apprentice on the first passageway—the labyrinth had been laid out in a crude way, I had already hollowed out the first little plaza, but its dimensions and the finish of the walls were inadequate; in short, everything was so much in its initial stages that it could only be accounted a trial, something that, when your patience gives out, you could abandon without any great regrets. Then, during one of the breaks in the work—all my life I allowed for far too many breaks in the work—I was lying among piles of soil and suddenly I heard a sound in the distance. Young as I was, I was more curious than frightened. I dropped my work and settled myself to listen, at least I knew to listen and wasn't running up to the moss to stretch my limbs and not hearing anything. At least I was listening. I could clearly tell that there was digging, like mine, a little feebler from the sound of it, but how much of that was attributable to the distance I couldn't tell. I was excited, but somehow remained calm. Perhaps I am in someone else's burrow, I thought, and the owner is on his way. If that had turned out to be the case, then I, who have never been aggressive or acquisitive, would have decamped, to build elsewhere. But remember I was still young and without a burrow of my own, so I could still be calm and collected. What happened next provoked no greater excitement; it was just hard to interpret. Assuming that the party digging, having been trying to get to me because he had heard me digging, was now changing direction, as he seemed to be doing, it wasn't easy to tell whether he was doing so because I, by stopping, had robbed him of his sense of direction, or if he had merely changed his mind. Perhaps I had deceived myself entirely, and he had never been making for me; at any rate the noise for a while grew louder, as though he was drawing nearer, and as a young person I might not even have been unhappy to see the digger suddenly rise up through the soil, but nothing of the sort happened; from a certain point on, the sound of digging began to weaken, it grew quieter and ever quieter, as though the digger had gradually changed direction, and eventually it stopped altogether, as though he had decided in favor of a completely different direction and was moving away from me into the distance. I listened for him in the silence for a long time before getting back to work. Well, the threat was clear enough, but soon enough I forgot all about it, and it barely had any effect on my building plans.

Between that time and the present I came to man's estate, but it still feels as though nothing has really happened, I still make great pauses in my work and listen at the wall, and the digger has again changed his intentions, he has turned tail, he is coming back from a journey, he thinks he has left me enough time to get ready to welcome him. But on my side, everything is even less prepared than it was then, the great burrow lies defenseless, and I am not a little apprentice any more, I am an old master builder and whatever strength I still have denies itself to me when it comes to making a decision. But however old I am, it seems to me that I wouldn't mind being older still, so old that I couldn't even get up from my billet under the moss. Because in reality I can't stand it here, I hurtle down into the burrow as though I had filled myself with fresh anxieties and not with calmness. What was the state of things now? Had the hissing got quieter? No, it had grown louder. I listen at ten random spots and my mistake is clear to me: the hissing has remained the same, nothing has changed. There are no changes over there; they are quiet and unworried about time, while here every instant jolts me, the listener. And I take the long way down to the citadel, everything around me seems in a state of turmoil, seems to be staring at me, seems to be avoiding my eye, so as not to disturb me, and then strains to read the saving intentions from my expression. I shake my head, I have none as yet. Nor do I go to the citadel to carry out any sort of plan. I pass the place where I was going to start digging the trench, I test it again, it would have been a good place, the trench would have gone in the direction where most of the little airshafts are, which would have greatly facilitated the work, perhaps I wouldn't even

have had to dig all that far, wouldn't have had to dig as far as
the source of the noise, perhaps further listening at the airshafts would have sufficed. But no thought is strong enough
to motivate me for this trench-digging. So this trench is to
give me certainty? I have reached a point where I don't even
want certainty. In the citadel I select a nice piece of skinned
red meat and crawl off onto one of the earth piles, there will
be silence there, inasmuch as there is any silence still to be
had anywhere. I lick and nibble at the meat, think by turns of
the strange animal making its way in the distance and then
of me and the time I have remaining to enjoy my stockpiles.
This last is probably the only realistic plan I have. Otherwise,
I am trying to second-guess the animal. Is it migrating or is it
working on its own burrow? If it's migrating, then it might be
possible to come to some accommodation with it. If it breaks
through into my terrain, then I can give it some of my provisions, and it will be on its way. Yes, it will want to be gone.
On my pile of earth I can of course dream of everything, even
of accommodation, even though I know for a fact that such
a thing is impossible and that the moment we clap eyes on
each other, yes, even the moment we sense one another's
proximity, both equally insensate, neither first, neither second, with a wholly new hunger, even if in other respects we
are completely satiated, we will bury our claws and teeth
into one another. And as ever, so here with all justification,
because even if he's migrating, who, in view of this burrow,
wouldn't change his plans? But maybe the animal is digging
in his own burrow, in which case I mustn't even dream of an
accommodation. Never mind that it's such an exotic animal
that its burrow would tolerate a neighbor, I know that mine
won't, at least not one within earshot. Now the animal admittedly seems to be very far off, if only it would withdraw

a little further, maybe the sound would disappear too, perhaps then everything would turn out as before, then it would
remain a grim but harmless experience, it would spur me
on to the varied improvements, when I have calm and am
no longer under the immediate press of danger, I am capable of quite respectable work. Maybe, given all the extraordinary possibilities of its technique, the animal will give up
and stop extending its burrow in the direction of mine, and
will compensate itself in the other direction. That too is not
something that can be arranged by negotiation, but purely by
the mind of the animal itself, or through some force exerted
from my side. Either way, what will be decisive is whether
and what the animal knows of me. The more I think about
it, the more unlikely it seems to me that the animal has even
heard me; it's possible, if hardly likely, that it has had some
news of me, without hearing me. As long as I hadn't known
about it, it won't have heard me at all, because I was keeping
quiet, there is nothing more quiet than the reunion with the
burrow; then, when I embarked on my relief trench, it might
have been able to hear me, even though my style of digging
is really terribly discreet; whereas if it had heard me, I surely
would have noticed something, it would have stopped in its
work from time to time to listen—but everything went on
unchanged—